2-

SALMON SURVIVOR

Christian A. Shane

SUTTON, ALASKA

Relevant Publishers LLC
P.O. Box 505
Sutton, AK 99674

www.relevantpublishers.com

Publisher's Cataloging-In-Publication Data

Names: Shane, Christian A., author.
Title: Salmon Survivor / written by Christian A. Shane
Description: Sutton, Alaska : Relevant Publishers, LLC, [2022] | Interest age level: 010-014. | Summary: "After the death of his father and fishing partner, twelve-year old Jack Cooper unwillingly travels with his mom from Pennsylvania to Alaska to meet his grandfather, Fly Bob, for the first time. Over the summer, Jack challenges himself to do something his father 'Redds' Cooper had never accomplished, catching the Alaskan Salmon Slam: all five species of Pacific salmon in one summer. Jack encounters more than he expected fly fishing on the waters of the Last Frontier. What does he uncover about his father's past? Will he repeat his dad's mistakes? While competing against the Alaskan wilderness, wildlife, and weather, can Jack complete the slam before the summer's end?"--Provided by publisher.

Identifiers: LCCN: 2022930001 | ISBN 978-1953263063 (paperback) | ISBN 978-1953263070 (ebook)

Subjects: LCSH: Salmon fishing--Alaska--Juvenile fiction. | Boys--Alaska--Juvenile fiction. | Fathers--Death--Psychological aspects--Juvenile fiction. | Grandfathers--Alaska--Juvenile fiction. | CYAC: Salmon fishing--Alaska--Fiction. | Boys--Alaska--Fiction. | Fathers--Death--Psychological aspects--Fiction. | Grandfathers--Alaska--Fiction.

Classification: LCC PZ7.1.S479 Sa 2022 (print) | LCC PZ7.1.S479 (ebook) | DDC [Fic]--dc23

Printed in the United States of America

DEDICATION

...for all those readers who have lost a loved one.

Hopefully, within your own time and healing,

your memories will be full of smiles rather than tears.

Table of Contents

PROLOGUE

SHADES OF GREEN, SHADOWS OF BLACK

The Elk Hair Caddis drifted smoothly on the stream's surface like a sailboat.

My dad hand tied the caddis using the hide hairs of a real Pennsylvania elk. The artificial fly's legs undulated on the water.

"He'll take it...just wait and see," Dad whispered.

This fly fishing game is all about stealth and patience. I controlled the fly line in the currents like Dad taught me and held my breath waiting for the fish to hit.

"I'm telling you, Jack-O, the bite is on. Can you feel it? Take another cast up there."

I set another cast upstream, and my fly flopped into the bubble line.

"Great cast, buddy. Right where you want it. Just a little longer...come on, eat it."

The fly floated under a large overhanging bush.

Slurp. Splash!

"Set, set, set," Dad got louder with each word.

I set the hook with a flick of my hand.

"Fish-on!" Dad's voice echoed through the valley.

"Fish-on!" I yelled back.

"He's a feisty one." I laughed and struggled to get him out of the currents.

As I reeled it into shore, Dad cradled the trout carefully in his hands.

Wormy lines created mazes along its back and colored spots spanned its body.

"Wow Jack, that is one beautiful Brookie," Dad beamed.

I took a picture as this would be one to remember. A trophy for us both.

Dad removed the fly from its mouth and held it in the current.

Then it tailed away into the shadows.

"Couldn't have done it better myself, boy! I'm really proud of you. You are one amazing angler."

"Hold your hand out," he said.

"Why?" I asked.

Dad turned my right palm downward and held it in his large hand.

"There, if you look down at just the right angle, you can make the shape of Alaska with your hand. We're headed to that little stretch on your thumb called the Kenai Peninsula."

I stretched my fingers out and imagined the state of Alaska fitting in my hand.

"Can't wait to catch some salmon with you, Jack!"

I couldn't wait, either.

There's nothing I wanted more than catching a salmon....

I was wrong.

CHAPTER 1

ALASKAN ☆
FACTS:

☆ ☆ ☆
☆   ☆
☆ ☆
☆

Alaska has more than 3,000 rivers &
more than 3 million lakes.

Salmon.

This was supposed to be an epic summer, a summer of catching fish.

My dad had already deemed it, "The Great Cooper Alaskan Salmon Slam."

Salmon.

I couldn't wait. My family would explore the mountains and rivers of Alaska together. Three generations of Coopers would fish for all five species. My dad, Redds Cooper, would finally achieve his lifelong dream of writing an Alaskan fishing guidebook and become nationally recognized. And me, I would finally meet my grandfather.

Salmon.

The word crashed over and over like waves in my skull.

Instead, Dad will never finish his book, and I have to spend the summer with a grumpy old man in waders.

This could be the worst summer of my life.

I've worked all month trying to get out of going on this trip. Tonight was my last chance, so I pleaded.

"Mom, can't we just tell him we're not coming?"

"Jack, I know it's hard to leave Pittsburgh for the summer, but everything's already planned, and your grandfather is looking forward to meeting you."

"Yeah right. Some grandfather. *Fly Bob* – what kind of name is that? He couldn't even fly down for the funeral. More like 'No-Fly Bob' if you ask me."

"Well, look on the bright side. You'll see some sights you've never seen before – the beautiful Alaskan scenery and wildlife. Plus, you can fish for salmon to your heart's content. Bob is really looking forward to meeting you and teaching you how to fish, Alaskan-style."

Another grown-up telling me what is good for me, just what I need.

"We shouldn't even give him the satisfaction of going up to visit him. He never took time to come down and see us."

As Mom washed the dishes, wearing jeans and Dad's old Penguins jersey, the kitchen light over the sink spotlighted her olive complexion. Her feathery brown ponytail swayed back and forth. We joked as a family that her hair was the same color as the elk hide we used to tie the caddis fly. Dad used his fingers, pretending to cut off her ponytail. He said that she shook it when she was extremely happy or on the verge of crying. I could tell which one it was tonight, but I still had to push.

"What if I stayed with Aunt Tinny and Uncle Max for the month? They wouldn't mind. Or maybe Charles', Peter's, or Ken's house?"

"Come on, Jack. You know this trip isn't easy for me, either. I want to finish what your dad started with his book. We are going to stay where he was born."

"...but Mom, I'm going to miss baseball camp. The guys will be so much better than me by the time school starts, and I'll miss the Kennywood picnic, too. This stinks!" I knew I was whining by this point, but I had to do something.

"Aren't you the least bit curious? Your dad was so excited for us to go on this adventure together, as a family."

"Dad's not here, and we're not a family anymore," I murmured.

The kitchen remained silent. I'd crossed the line.

She ignored the comment and continued drying the dishes without giving me the look, yet I could feel her blue eyes locking with mine.

"Well, unless you plan on wearing the same clothes for a month, I suggest you get to packing. We're leaving for the airport tomorrow at five AM."

"Whatever." I shoved the chair and stormed out the back door.

The gray clouds blanketing the sky reflected my dismal mood. Trudging to the rusty red shed out behind our house, I grabbed Dad's vest, camo hat, and bamboo fly rod. Then I filled my backpack with fly gear and headed to the stream.

The valley provided the usual lush green sights Dad and I enjoyed every summer. Enormous evergreens still towered over the forest floor supplying coolness and shade. Lime green ferns lined the trailhead like lights on an airport runway, and the water rushing below drowned out the bird calls from high above. I inhaled a full breath of pine and sighed.

The bamboo rod bounced on my shoulder as I tramped down the trailhead path, but I couldn't stomp away the fact that Mom wouldn't budge on this one. We were headed to the forty-ninth state without my dad. She thought it would be good for us both to get a change of scenery, and my opinion didn't seem to matter.

Boots squishing into the mud, I paused at the trail's end, closed my eyes, and focused on the sounds of the creek. Dad's trick to cooling off. But even the rushing water sounded flat this time, like when my buddy, Denny, played his guitar out of tune.

I sat on the gigantic boulder that Dad and I'd nicknamed Table Rock, thinking of all the times we'd eaten lunch and recapped the day's fishing. Then I reached into the pack for my fishing journal and unfolded the newspaper clipping:

COOPER, JOHN ROBERT "Redds"
Age 46,
of Pittsburgh, Pennsylvania, died on April 21,
of an accidental drowning in Slippery Rock
Creek.

Son of the late Judy Cooper. Survived by his
father Robert "Fly Bob" Cooper, beloved
husband to Jillian Cooper, and loving father to
Jack Cooper.

Redds worked over 20 years as an outdoor
writer for the **Pennsylvania Outdoor Gazette**.
He was an avid fly fisherman, author, gardener,
hunter, guide, and conservationist.

Donations can be made in his name to the
"Save Our Wild Salmon Coalition" and Trout
Unlimited. Send condolences to
www.pennsylvaniaoutdoorgazette.com/cooper

Most people called my dad "Redds." He had the best job I could imagine - an outdoor news writer. All through the state of Pennsylvania, outdoor enthusiasts, hunters and fishermen knew "Redds" for his articles and news stories related to the environment. He pretty much wrote the guide on fishing in Pennsylvania. And he got to teach families how to fish and even spoke at outdoor events about fly fishing and fly tying. He was always helping people.

I was one of his biggest fans, tagging along on his excursions and adventures whenever I had time off from school, especially in the summers. Dad always said, "Nature is the perfect classroom for a kid."

Don't be fooled, though, nature is cruel.

My dad could wade almost anywhere, the safest and smartest wader I know. He was a stout guy with a football-type frame having tree trunks for legs both in and out of the water. His fishing buddies called him Sasquatch because he was six foot, three inches and had a big hairy beard and somewhat balding head. He even had a bumper sticker on his truck with a furry Yeti holding a giant rainbow trout. I figured someday, I'd be as tall as him, but

I'm still growing at twelve, not even six foot yet. Everyone says I look like him, but I don't see the resemblance.

Still, I was one of the taller kids in my class last year. And though I couldn't wade in higher waters like him, I still held my own in the currents and wasn't afraid. Besides, we had durable wading boots worn over our chest waders that kept us dry and warm all the way to our elbows.

"Don't ever underestimate the power of water," Dad always warned. "Never wade above the top of your chest waders, or the water will flow in and take you to the bottom." We even wore belts around our waists as a precaution of water rushing in, so we rarely waded in anything over our hips, and we *always* respected the water.

I should've been fishing with him the day that he drowned. If I'd been with him, maybe he wouldn't have waded in tough waters.

How could he be so stupid wading in high water? How could he do this to me?

On that April morning, I'd overheard my parents talking in the kitchen.

"Be careful, Redds. It's been raining for three days straight. Won't the water be too high?"

"I'll be OK, Honey...I'll stay close to the banks. Fished it a million times, no worries."

I waited up in bed as long as I could for him that night. I couldn't wait to hear how the bite was even in all that high water. Mom woke me in a panic and said to come downstairs.

I still see water puddling around the boots of the two State Police officers who sat soaking in our living room that rainy morning telling us my dad had drowned.

The questions flooded in:

What went wrong? How did it happen?

Did he slip?

Did he get stuck under one of those boulders?

...Did he suffer?

I reread the obituary and felt my limbs go numb; it's been three months, and I can't believe he's gone.

How many times did we compare notes about the weather, the water, the bugs, the fish? I turned to my journal, just a piece of history now, our history together.

I opened the book and found the last time I added an entry; it was April, and we'd just started fishing. How quickly three months go by.

I can see that day in my mind as if it's at the bottom of a clear stream:

DAY: April 1st

TIME: 7:43 a.m.

STREAM: Little Scrubgrass

WEATHER: Kind of cloudy, sun is peeking through

AIR TEMP: 66 degrees

WATER TEMP: 58 degrees

FLY: Elk Hair Caddis

NOTES: April Fool's Day. I hope I can fool a brook trout into taking my fly. Dad tied up a new caddis pattern that we're using today. Nothing yet, but the water looks perfect.

I flipped a page in the fishing journal and strained to write an entry. Seemed pointless now that I didn't have him to talk fishing. If ever there was a place to cheer up and feel closest to him, it's down here at the creek.

I could almost hear him telling me to *'Be tough'* and *'Stick it out'* without him there.

OK, Cooper, concentrate on the fishing checklist. Water temperature? Air temperature? Water clarity? Any bug activity? I studied the currents as the hidden sun splashed shadows on the water's surface. A few bugs in the Big Hole.

I leaned over and dipped in my hand to check the water temp, a little warm for this time of year. My reflection reminded me I hadn't cut my hair since Dad died. No wonder Mom was calling me a Wookie lately. I glanced down at my clothes: a plain gray t-shirt, camouflage pants with pockets and Dad's tan fishing vest. Dull enough. Last summer at this time, I'd worn my white Steelers jersey and scared away every fish in the pool before I could even make a cast.

"Jack-O, in order to catch a trout, you've got to blend in with your surroundings. Think like a trout." I remember Dad saying, puffing on his pipe and smiling.

This time, I blend.

When an enormous shadow darted across the flat pool and hid near a rock for cover, I shifted slowly to the left. *There, a better glimpse of it.* The white edges along its bottom fin revealed a large brook trout hiding among the rocks, the perfect camouflage. It had to be at least sixteen inches, an excellent specimen. Dad would die for a fish like this one.

Stupid thing to think.

I opened the fly box, and the familiar pipe scent wafted up. Plucking out the familiar bushy, buggy Elk Hair Caddis fly, I reluctantly knotted the fly to the end of my line.

I'd practiced this more times than spots on a trout. Plop the fly on the water's surface like a real caddis. As the fish rises to the water's surface to snatch it, set the hook. Nothing to it. Just like before.

Before Dad died.

Seeing my movement, the trout bolted across the pool and camouflaged itself on the gravel bottom.

Usually, I'm the first one to the stream and the one to make the first cast. "You are one impatient angler," Dad always laughed.

But not here. Not today.

The trout recovered its energy and rested at the bottom of the stream. The fish struggled to suck oxygen out of the warming water, and I mimicked the fish opening and closing his mouth.

Out of breath.

I lost my best friend.

My chest tightened.

Like a fish breathing for water.

I hoped my thoughts would echo through the valley to Dad.

To make matters worse, I would have to travel with Mom tomorrow to a place I had never been before to meet a grandfather I'd never known.

CHAPTER 2

ALASKAN ☆
FACTS:

☆ ☆ ☆ ☆
☆
☆ ☆

**The Alaskan State Flag is
blue with yellow stars
in the shape of the Big Dipper.**

"How's the new journal going?" Mom asked me as the pilot turned off the 'no seat belts' sign.

From under the brim of Dad's camo hat and leaning my legs up against the seat back, I gave Mom a blank stare. "Fine." I went back to scribbling my hand in the shape of Alaska.

This new journal had been her idea. Before the trip, she mentioned it would be "healthy" for me to start a fresh journal to write down my feelings and mark the summer trip. I'm guessing she gave Fly Bob the idea of mailing me the new journal before we left. Probably trying to win me over before we met. *Fat chance*: he didn't even write a note in it.

I liked the cover though, a field of navy blue, dotted with yellow stars in the pattern of the Big Dipper – the Alaska State flag.

Very clever.

Under normal circumstances, I enjoyed writing in a fishing journal. Ever since I could write full sentences, Dad and I had kept a fishing journal to mark the trip and compare notes every time we went out on the water. We'd take the water temperature, cite weather details, and note the flies we used to lure hungry trout. In school, I sometimes hid the fishing journal among my folders so I could write in it whenever I had free time in class. I loved to design fly patterns for us to tie up and try on the water. I would list the flies we used, where we caught them, and any other fun things we saw along the stream that day. I daydreamed of streams teeming with bugs on the surface and the trout gorging on them.

Dad was gone, and two of my favorite things were disappearing along with him – my love of writing and fishing.

During the two flights from Pennsylvania to Anchorage, Mom tried to talk, but I didn't budge. She forced me to go on this trip, and I hoped she'd regret ever bringing me along.

Mom attempted again.

"Hey Jack, will you help me finish your Dad's book? I really want this Alaskan Guide to be a tribute to your father. It's practically done anyway."

This was Mom's excuse for sticking with the trip to Alaska even without Dad. He had only one major river system left to finish his Alaskan Guidebook on salmon fishing, the Kenai River where he grew up. He'd taken so many trips in the last few years without us that I wasn't sure why he didn't just stop by the last time he was up there, probably to avoid Fly Bob.

Mom worked as a journalist and photographer for the local newspaper, but she rarely picked up a rod and admitted to having very little interest in fly fishing. Still, she supported Dad's goal of creating the Alaskan Guide.

I scoffed, "You don't even fish anymore."

"Well, I figured between Fly Bob and the other guides, I'll learn about Alaska and finish the book. It's my way of saying goodbye to your dad. Maybe you'll find something to do in your dad's memory on this trip, too."

Mom leaned her head against the plane window and stared down at the icy mountains. The captain turned the 'fasten seat belt' sign back on, and my stomach sank deeper and deeper as the plane descended. To distract myself, I pulled out the Alaskan itinerary which Dad left on his desk.

Right before leaving on the trip, I'd poked around in his den and found all the Alaska information, including the itinerary. He'd listed a rough sketch of what he wanted to accomplish while in Alaska.

SALMON SURVIVOR

ALASKA ITINERARY

July 4 - Depart Pittsburgh, PA/Arrive Detroit,
    MI, Depart Detroit, MI/Arrive
    Anchorage, Overnight in Anchorage

July 5 - Alaskan Railroad to Kenai Peninsula,
    Grandview Station, Bus line from Seward Highway to Cooper Landing,
    Meet Dad/Unpack at Cabins

July 6-8 - Russian River Ferry/Fishing/Hiking/Sightseeing/
    Kings/Sockeye

July 9-13 - Soldotna/Homer/Hatchery

July 13-18 - Chum Runs/Kenai River drift

July 19-23 - Hiking, Kayaking, Seward, Kenai Fjords trip

July 24-29 - Pinks/Silvers in? Rainbows, Dollies

July 30 - Train/Travel back to Anchorage/hotel

July 31 - Depart Anchorage/Arrive Salt Lake City, UT,
    Depart Salt Lake City, UT/Arrive Pittsburgh
    HOME SWEET HOME

How much of this will we even get to do now?

The flight attendants came around for a seatbelt check as we descended into cloudy Anchorage. Giant snow-capped mountains on the left side of the plane loomed large as we touched down on the runway.

After a less-than-smooth landing, the captain said, "Hello everyone. We'd like to welcome you to the Forty-Ninth State. The current weather in Anchorage, Alaska is fifty-seven degrees and cloudy. On behalf of the crew, thanks for flying Alaskan Airlines, and we hope you enjoy your stay in Alaska."

I rolled my eyes.

As we walked out of the plane down the connector, I noticed the airport looked a lot like Pittsburgh's, except a lot of realistically posed animals were spread out along the airport like a creepy museum. Walking to baggage, Mom and I stopped at a huge moose with a large rack.

I noticed a few different types of bears (Kodiak, Black, and Grizzly), a bunch of geese sculptures, and a helicopter hanging high between the words "Welcome to Alaska," right where we were supposed to get our baggage.

Mom had tied these rainbow fishing bandanas to our luggage, and we spotted the spectrum of colors dotted with black right away among the heaps of suitcases. They were all Dad's. He used them to keep the sun off his head and neck, and now we use them for luggage recognizers. At least I kept Dad's favorite Brook Trout bandana with my fishing gear for the right purpose.

We each collected a duffel bag and shuttled over to the downtown Anchorage hotel. The town wasn't what I expected. Way too flat and a little touristy with all its souvenir shops, buses, guide tours, and flowers blooming everywhere. It reminded me of Disney World rather than a rugged place.

Where were the bears, moose, and rivers that Dad talked up? What made him so excited about visiting this place?

My face burned as I wondered what it would be like if Dad were here. Probably cracking some jokes. Maybe something like, "Not sure where our hotel is, your Mom knows, maybe Al-ask-ha." Or maybe, "Jack and Jill went up the hill to catch a little salmon..." He always could make us smile.

The white-covered mountains towered over the landscape, distracting me now since they looked so much closer on the ground. It was late in the evening, but the sun still hung over the horizon. I guessed it was around about 9:00 p.m.

I looked at my watch, *11:05 p.m.* A trout secondhand clicked around the numbers on my silver watch face. Mom and Dad had bought me the fishing watch on my twelfth birthday, right before he died.

Wish I could turn back the hands of time.

The hotel was near the airport, around the area of what they call Earthquake Park. With moose heads on the walls, stuffed animals everywhere, and framed pictures of orca whale pods and whale tails, it seems they really like their wildlife up here in Alaska.

Inside, we ate at a restaurant named 'Humpy's' with a big humpbacked salmon underneath the letters. Mom had a salmon salad, and I ordered a regular old cheeseburger called the 'Anchorage Special' with everything on it.

After chowing down, I yawned with exhaustion. We still had one last leg of the trip tomorrow, south on the Alaskan Railroad to meet Fly Bob.

We settled into the hotel room and crawled into our beds. In Pittsburgh, it would be 3:00 a.m., but I was wide awake. Maybe because it's still light out. *Too much time to think.*

A loud booming sound came from outside the window.

BOOM, CRACK-OW, BOOM!

I'd totally forgot it's the Fourth of July!

Dad had made such a big deal about flying across the country on Independence Day.

Big deal. Today was just another day.

I peeked through the blinds and barely made out the fireworks in downtown Anchorage off in the distance. Over the horizon, I imagined the star pattern of the Big Dipper hanging in the sky and its giant spoon pouring the red, green, and yellow fireworks onto the mountainous landscape.

Same as the journal cover.

JA-BOOM, JA-BOOM, PFFFFFF. BOOM!

I jumped back in bed and tried to ignore the sounds. Mom shut off the lights, but it was still as bright as ever.

BA-BOOM, PFFFFFF. BA-BOOM!

"Mommmmm," I whispered over to her. "Are you still awake?"

"How can I sleep with all this noise?" She turned over in her bed and then climbed over into mine. We laid there staring at the ceiling and listened for the next explosion.

BA-BA-BOOM, BA-BA-BOOM!

"Hey Jack, I have an idea for your Alaskan journal. Why not draft some letters to your father? Keep a log for him of everything we're doing this month. That would be amazing. You know he would've appreciated that. Maybe we can even include it somehow in the book."

"Yeah, maybe." She squeezed my clenched fist.

Mom's voice cracked. "I miss him so much."

"Me too," I held it together even though I was melting next to her.

"I'm always here for you, Jack." She wiped her eyes on my cuff. "You can talk about anything with me. Remember that." Brushing the hair out of my eyes, she said, "Remember that. We'll be here for each other."

Mom kissed me on the forehead and returned to her bed. She crashed into sleep and started to snore. I regretted treating her so mean during the start of this trip. I knew this was a gut punch for her, too.

I opened the Alaskan journal.

With the fireworks exploding in the distance, I started my first letter to Dad:

July 4th - 11:30 p.m.

Dear Dad,

Wow, I miss you so much it hurts. We've finally made it to Alaska, but I'm not really happy without you here. There are fireworks going off in the daylight. Can you believe it? The sounds remind me of the Fourth of July when we watched the fireworks on the Ohio River bridge back home. Remember we sat and watched the fireworks explode over Pittsburgh? They were the best.

I'm kind of nervous about tomorrow. We're taking the train to meet your dad. I hope he's like you.

Anyway, good night and know that I'm thinking of you, always.

As the last few Alaskan fireworks ended, I lay wide awake and remembered watching them with my family on that bridge.

CHAPTER 3

We walked out of the hotel to a brisk, blue-sky morning. Denali stood far off in the distance, and even from a couple hundred miles away, it shouldered over the horizon, like a postcard picture. Dad shared that "it makes its own weather," and the Koyukon Athabascans originally named it 'Denali,' meaning "the High One." The mountain had been renamed Mt. McKinley for years, but thankfully, it had returned to its original name. Too bad we're going south on the Alaskan railroad, the opposite way, to meet Fly Bob.

We left for the Anchorage train station at 7:00 a.m. When we arrived, the enormous blue and yellow cars of the Alaskan Railroad loomed over me. Two train engines led the twelve connected passenger rail cars, each with huge glass-wrapped windows.

This was my first train ride ever, so I imagined I was an old Alaskan gold prospector on the way to new territories. Outside the station, I studied the large topographical map of Alaska. We would travel south from Anchorage to the Grandview Junction station on the Kenai Peninsula of Alaska, then drive west a short distance along the Kenai River to milepost fifty, the town of Cooper Landing.

"Made it in time! Ready?" Mom waved the train tickets.

I galloped ahead to board the train. With Dad's old backpack in hand, I stepped back in time as I entered the rail car and walked up narrow steps to find my seat.

"Wow, someone's excited!"

I still didn't want her to think she had won, so I stuck out my tongue. Dad wasn't here, and I couldn't be mannerly. I imagined him trying to fit his body through the train's skinny aisles, bumping into every armrest like he always did on planes.

Mom found our seats, and I flopped into the chair next to the enormous domed windows. On the train platform, I noticed a little boy about six-years-old. He was waving "moose ears" at me, so I put my thumbs above my ears and waved "moose ears" back. Maybe this is a weird way of saying hello in Alaskan?

The engine let out a mighty whistle, and the train lunged forward. Soon the train cars followed in line, and we picked up speed moving down the track. We followed the Turnagain Arm, where the steep mountains seemed to plummet into the water.

The plush seats and wrap-around scenery made me feel like I was in a gigantic movie theater.

Right away, my eagle eyes (as Dad called them) spotted the first sign of wildlife.

"Look Mom, a moose!" I cried, pointing out the left dome window standing near the tracks. The other passengers rushed to that side of the train to confirm the moose sighting.

There are moose this close to Anchorage?

The moose locked eyes with me for a split second as the train gained momentum. I observed every detail: its elongated rack, its broad shoulders, its thick coat of fur, eyes as black as coal.

Dad would love this.

After spotting a bald eagle's nest, some sheep, and another moose in the distance, I did a little exploring around the train and let the other passengers spot their own wildlife for a while. Mom leaned on a pillow against the window, fast asleep in her seat, so I let her be.

The narrow staircase led to the lower floor. A sign attached to the door read:

> ## USE CAUTION
> ## WHEN CROSSING OVER
> ## TO THE NEXT TRAIN CAR

As I opened the railcar door, a gust of wind blasted me, nearly knocking Dad's camo hat off my head.

A conductor stood on a small platform connecting the two cars. He leaned against a gate on the metal platform which attached the cars. The scenery rushed by at high speed. No windows down here.

"It's a little windy out here, kid, but if you can take it, it's the best spot on the train." The conductor smiled. "Just be careful. Don't want to lose any passengers!"

I hesitated before walking to the railing and peering down at the tracks. As the rails sped underneath, the train's wheels screeched like bats, and the dust kicked up all around.

Wow, I couldn't believe they let passengers do this.

I felt like a dog who'd stuck his head out of the car window to sniff the breeze, only this wind was gale force. I turned my head toward the back of the train and breathed in the brisk Alaskan air. With my eyes closed, I filled my lungs till my chest bulged. Now that's fresh air.

Out in the distance, I marveled at the enormous snow-capped mountain ranges against the vast blue sky and the tide rolling in.

"A lot of tourists come up here, but not many people get a chance to see a robin-egg blue sky." The conductor lamented.

"Yeah," I shared. "We got a chance to see Denali outside of our hotel this morning. Pretty cool."

"Wow. Usually, the clouds cover Denali's peak. We say if you can see the summit on a clear day, you'll have luck for the summer. You must be lucky, kid."

"Sure." I nodded politely.

"Enjoy your Alaskan adventure." The conductor winked, opened the sliding door, and disappeared into the next train car.

Mom finally found me in the conductor's spot and coaxed me into getting some lunch. Suddenly, my stomach growled at me. It's the same with fly fishing. Dad and I could stay out on the water all day without eating until we realized that our stomachs had started to rumble.

The fishing bug could do that to you. Maybe the Alaskan bug is like that, too.

In the lower dining car, we continued to enjoy the moving scenery but from a different perspective now. Things slowed down a bit. As the train wound around every corner, I examined the glacial waters adjacent the train tracks.

A debris field of logs, rocks and plants churned in the gray matter. Some fishermen lined the banks and cast their lines into the murky water.

Would Dad be dumb enough to wade into that river, too? What fish is worth that?

The grayish tint and discoloration of the silty water made it mysterious and mesmerizing, luring me back to thoughts of fishing.

Mom ordered me an egg sandwich and a Lenny's 'Laskan Root Beer.

With my mouth full, I asked Mom, "I hup we git into sum fith."

She gave me that "don't-talk-with-your-mouth-full" stare and waited for me to swallow and wash it down with root beer.

"Sorry...I hope we get into some fish."

"Ha ha, Jack, your father shared that Cooper Landing is the center of the universe when it comes to salmon fishing. I'm *sure* Fly Bob will get you into some fish."

"Maybe," I speculated.

"So, what are you going to call him?" she questioned.

It caught me off guard. My mom's parents lived north of us in Erie, and I called them 'Mom-mom' and 'Pop-pop.' I never thought that I would meet Dad's dad since they didn't talk with each other. Mom always told me not to push it since his family splitting up was a sore subject for Dad. Recently, when Dad was working on the Alaskan Guide, I started learning bits and pieces about his family, especially Fly Bob.

"I think I'll stick with Bob or *Old Man*." I answered.

"Jack, we have to give him a chance. It's what your dad would've wanted."

Mom was right. Dad's theme recently was "mending fences," as if they were something our family was building. I wondered what it took for families not to talk to each other anymore.

"But Dad hated him," I countered.

"No, not true. Your father loved Bob. They just didn't know how to go about making up for past mistakes. We're going there to finish what your father wanted. He really wanted Fly Bob to be a part of our lives and to let go of the past."

Yeah, mend the fences, right.

"I'm headed up to the gift shop to get some Alaskan souvenirs. Want anything special?" Mom asked.

"Nope. Already have one." I sarcastically waved my journal.

Alone, I sat in the lunchroom car and swiped through my cell phone gallery to remind myself of happier times before Dad died. One picture I really liked of Mom and Dad together.

Mom's birthday fell on the baseball home opener that year, so we went to the ballpark to celebrate. Mom's favorite player, Cutch, hit a three-run homer, and it landed in our section. Dad reached out and snagged it. I took a picture of my mom smiling and my dad holding up the ball.

The last picture I had of Dad alive was holding that beautiful brook trout. The bright sun lit him up from behind and made him look like an angel. I should've known that day would be a special memory.

Not many pics of Pittsburgh to share after that one. Not too many memory-worthy pictures to take. Wonder if Alaska will have something better. That reminded me of Fly Bob's picture.

Before leaving Pennsylvania, I took our only picture of my dad's dad out of the frame and taped it into my journal. Not sure why I did that, guess I wanted to start getting to know him. It was of Fly Bob holding an enormous fish, a salmon. I pulled out my journal and flipped to the back-cover picture.

Thick glasses sat on the face of the bearded man wearing layers upon layers of clothing and a camouflage jacket holding it all in. His camo blended right into his darker waders. He seemed shorter than Dad, as he stood there with a smirk, holding an enormous silvery fish by its gills. His bearded face looked a little like Dad's, but more rugged, thin, and worn out. He looked extremely sad behind his smile.

In all my time with Dad, he never mentioned much about Fly Bob. I did some investigating on Fly Bob before this trip. While searching around in Dad's den, I found all the letters and pictures Fly Bob had sent Dad.

In the most recent letter, Fly Bob spilled his guts to Dad. He handwrote the note and said things like "I'm sorry;" "I shoulda been there for you and your family;" "I've made many mistakes;" and "I want to make it up to you." I guess Dad felt it was enough to bring us all out here to make up with Fly Bob. Now, he'll never get the chance.

Fly Bob promised he would show us a good time on the water and give us the ins-and-outs of salmon fishing. I guess he's some well-known guide up in Cooper Landing, and Dad wanted his help to finish the Alaskan Fly Fishing Guide. Dad said he "saved the best for last," describing the Kenai River area in his guidebook. I wondered if he'd still keep his promise without Dad here.

What would Fly Bob be like? Why didn't Dad talk about him much? Why didn't Fly Bob show up to the funeral of his own son?

So many unanswered questions.

I took the last swig of my Lenny's 'Laskan Root Beer and thought back to the quote Dad had hanging on his office wall.

"It's not called catchin'. It's called fishin'. Nothing comes easy."

Especially in Alaska.

Arriving at the Alaskan Railroad Grandview Station with the Kenai Mountain range towering around us, we took what they called 'The Bus Line' (more like a small van) and followed the Sterling Highway to Cooper Landing.

Pennsylvania had mountains, rivers, and streams, but this Alaskan land seemed prehistoric with its overgrown trees and pockets of deep mysterious water. Around every curve in the road, the snow-covered mountains loomed, the calm waters below reflecting them in shadows of jade. Scents from the spruce trees penetrated the van, filling the vehicle like a natural air freshener. As the road snaked beside the Kenai River, I watched it flow like liquid turquoise. The land on all sides spoke to me in a whisper.

My stomach did Alaskan cartwheels. I knew this ride would lead to Fly Bob.

The van stopped outside a restaurant with a sign above that read *Gwin's Lodge*. The bearded man with thick glasses in hip waders standing under the restaurant sign greeted us. Wearing an old Pirates baseball hat, an older version of Dad stood there, but shorter, stockier, and grizzlier.

There he was at last. I'd been waiting my whole life to meet this guy.

Why am I so nervous?

My stomach tightened like the clinch knot at the end of my fishing line.

"Howdy. Welcome to my neck of the woods!"

Fly Bob rushed to give Mom a bear hug.

"It's been a long time, Jill." My mother disappeared in his embrace, her thin frame swallowed by his arms.

"Too long, Bob," she smiled with tears in her eyes. They hugged for an uncomfortable amount of time.

"...and I suppose this young man is the famous Jack? Well, welcome to Cooper Landing! It's good to finally meet you."

Does he want me to clap?

"He's really looking forward to fishing with you. Right, Jack?" My mom said, nudging me.

"Um, yeah," My palms sweated, and I wiped them on my pant legs.

Fly Bob reached out with two hands to shake my one hand. Something Dad used to do.

"So, did you see the three M's yet?"

OK, I'll play along. "No, what are those?"

"Didja see a moose yet?"

"Yep."

"Didja see the mountains?"

"Yep."

"Didja see any mosquitoes?"

"Yep." I rubbed my hand over the bumps on my arm to prove it. Alaskan mosquitoes were monsters.

"Well, there ya go. You've seen the three M's of Alaska. You might as well go home since the best part is over."

That sounds about right.

I spotted a creature approaching at full speed.

Too late to move. This is it! My first bear attack.

The monster barreled me off my feet, and we both tumbled to the ground. Next, a wet sensation slurped my cheek and a sandpaper-like tongue covered my face.

"Down girl." Bob patted the grungy grayish-white dog on the head as it moved to sit at attention beside him.

I reached over and read the metal tag on her collar. "S-A-L-M-O... *Sal-Mo.*"

"Ha, ha, you're close. She's named after the salmon, aren't you, Samo? The silent 'L' always gets the greenhorns. I rescued her from around Denali National Park. She used to be an old Alaskan sled dog. Now, I think she's just happy to be the Cooper Landing mascot!"

Salmo seemed to grin at the mention of her name.

I rubbed her thick and gnarled coat of fur, and Salmo returned the favor with a tail wag, my first Alaskan friend.

"Now let's drop off your luggage at the cabin, and if you guys are hungry, we can get some grub. I make the restaurant's best Salmon Chowder Soup and just so happened to whip up a fresh batch this morning."

"We rarely give up a chance to eat seafood, let's go!" Mom spoke for both of us.

She continued to break the awkwardness for all of us by asking questions.

"So Bob, didn't you mention owning some of this land?"

Fly Bob pointed all around at the scenery, "Yeah, my great grandpap used to own all of this. In fact, they ended up naming the whole town after him around the early 1900's. He and his wife, Gwin, moved up here and lived where the restaurant now is. After many years of selling it off bit by bit, now we just have a few cabins around this fire pit and own some of the restaurant. But hey, I still got my trailer and this beautiful country, so I can't complain. Here's your home away from home for the month."

He walked up the wooden steps to a small rustic log cabin. It was one of six cabins. A large wooden fish with a red head and green body hung over the entrance.

"It's the best cabin of all in these parts, and I saved it especially for you guys because it has running water."

Why didn't the other cabins have running water?

We walked in and saw a small living area, a kitchenette, a bedroom, a ladder that led upstairs a bed, and a functional bathroom.

"I guess that loft is for the boy." Fly Bob gestured for me to climb the ladder. I took a quick peek.

After dropping off our bags and gear in the cabin, we took the short gravel trail over to Bob's trailer behind the cabins. He tied Salmo out front on a chain. The aroma of the restaurant filled the evening air. We followed the fried smells to the restaurant on the main road while Salmo stayed behind.

Stepping inside reminded me of the diner back home, a place where Dad and I ate often, but this place was unique. Colossal fish hung high on the walls, real fish or replicas, I wasn't sure. Antique rods, reels, and nets dangled from the ceiling. The scent of greasy food mixed with a stench of wet clothes stung my nose.

I listened to all the conversations in the restaurant. At the corner table sat some fishing guides discussing their catches and misses. A mom and dad in the far-right corner laughed with their two little boys while eating chicken strips. Two backpackers argued over a map spread out on their table in the middle of the restaurant.

A girl around my age, maybe older, sat alone in one of the booths reading the menu. She still had her waders and boots on. Her fly rod was strung up next to the booth. She wore a tie-dyed hoodie with a wolf on it and had brown braided pigtails sticking out from a YETI hat. Her cheeks were rosy, maybe wind burned, but I thought she was pretty in a rugged sort of way. I may have stared at her just a little too long as she caught my gaze, and I quickly looked away.

"Come on in, honey. Welcome to the Lodge. Don't be shy." A friendly waitress with tattoos on her arms and neck led me inside. She had a long brunette braid, rosy cheeks, and wore a tank top that said: "Gwin's Lodge – Home of the Halibut Burger."

"My name's Kim. What's yours?"

"I'm Jack...from Pittsburgh."

"Well, Jack from Pittsburgh, it's good to have ya here in Cooper Landing. So hey, you must be Fly Bob's grandson?"

I nodded.

"Bob's been lookin' forward to having you and your mom for a while. Wow, you look so much like Redds, same hair and everything! Gosh, I had such a crush on him when I was a teenager."

Kim stammered a bit and tried to recover. "We're all really sorry for the loss of your dad. Some of us are old enough to remember him, even ole' Ace here."

She pointed over to an older guy sitting at the bar.

"Thanks." I replied politely, especially genuine to those who acknowledged Dad's passing.

Then the old man glanced up from his meal and noticed me standing there.

"Hey Redds, come on over here. Lemme get a good look at you. It's been too long. Whereya been? Did you bring any of those flies?"

Did he just call me Redds?

"Ah, don't mind ole' Ace, he's a regular here at the Lodge. All these old salmon river rats hang out here. He's usually harassing us waitresses."

Ace's long lips slowly gobbled up his salad, resembling the moose head which hung over the bar. He mumbled about fly patterns and then turned his attention back to the TV.

"Redds was a great guy." Kim sighed. "I think there's a few pictures of him around the restaurant here. You should go try to find them."

I scanned the room and saw hundreds of framed photos of fishermen.

"I have a daughter around your age over there. Maybe she'll show you a little of the restaurant and Cooper Landing this summer, too."

I pretended not to notice where Kim pointed and looked everywhere else but the girl's booth. Now that she mentioned it, they looked like they were related.

Kim led me over to Mom and Fly Bob at the table.

It was weird seeing them share stories together. Mom was pretending to know Fly Bob so well. It was sickening that she was acting so nice to him. She's so forgiving sometimes. Not me, he was going to have to work all summer for my forgiveness.

So I kept to myself, zoned out, and stared at the paper placemats.

Each placemat had a different fact about Alaska. There must have been at least fifty facts. I read all the placemats on the table to myself while Mom and Fly Bob droned on.

I ripped off a few facts and slid them into my journal.

The state of Rhode Island could fit into Alaska 425 times.

Alaska has more coastline than the rest of the United States, roughly 34,000 miles.

Alaska's name is derived from the Aleut word 'Alaxsxaq' meaning 'main land' and is known as Alyeska, 'the great land.'

It gave me a reason not to have to talk. At least Gwin's had Lenny's 'Laskan Root Beer on the menu.

After dinner, we headed back to the cabin and went to bed pretty early. It was still light out at 10:00 p.m.

Better get used to these long summer nights in Alaska.

CHAPTER 4

July 6th — 9:10 a.m.

Dear Dad,

Sorry I didn't write much yesterday. We had a busy travel day.

We're here in Cooper Landing. Weird to be in a town named after our family. I'm seeing our last name everywhere — fly shops, gas stations, laundromats, and even a library. I finally met Fly Bob.

Our cabin is pretty cool, and the restaurant nearby has some great food. I had a halibut burger last night — man was that good. I wonder if they cooked those up when you were a kid. Did they have the paper placemats with the Alaska facts when you were here? I haven't found one that repeated a fact, yet.

"Hello Coopers. You just made it to breakfast before the switch over," Kim the waitress shared. "Fly Bob also left you some presents at the booth."

The jet lag was torture for us. With the time difference from Pittsburgh to Alaska, it was hard for us to wake up, so we'd slept in a little. I noticed Fly Bob back in the kitchen helping out with the cooking. He gave us a wave through the kitchen take-out window.

Kim walked us to the booth, and salmon flies were scattered all over the table.

More presents from Fly Bob, probably to butter me up.

I pushed them over to the side of the booth and looked at my placemat to find new Alaskan facts.

Much of Alaska, including the state capital, is only accessible by boat or plane.

As the largest state in the United States, Alaska is approximately one-fifth the size of the continental United States.

Alaskan residents do not pay sales or income tax but receive an annual dividend check from oil sales.

Still no repeats.

Mom picked up a bright fly. "Wow, these are neat flies. A lot bigger than you guys use at home, right."

I just grunt.

"Mornin.' I see you found the flies," said Fly Bob, picking up one from the pile. "This one's called the Flash Fly, one of my favorites."

It was tied on a large salmon-curved hook with red feathers in the front and silver Mylar tinsel wrapped along a shank. Probably supposed to look like a minnow or something.

"I like this one," Mom chose, handling another.

I kept reading the placemats.

"Ah, that's called 'Cotton Candy.' The fish go crazy after that one. They look good enough to eat."

I took a quick peek as Fly Bob tied one on his vise, using bright red thread to fasten the furry pink chenille. The Cotton Candy fly has tufts of white on its ends and a pink body cinched in the middle. It looks like a pink tootsie roll. Man, these salmon really like the bright flies. In Pennsylvania, we tie more natural looking colors on our flies.

"This one imitates the salmon flesh," Fly Bob commented as he knotted the fly and snipped at the thread with his scissors.

Salmon flesh, great breakfast conversation.

"What are you getting to eat, Jack?" Mom asks, feathering the fly material across her palm.

"The crab omelet is my favorite,' he said, "and don't forget the hash browns."

Kim took our order.

Mom got the crab omelet and hash browns.

I ordered the waffles.

"I still can't get over how much Jack looks like Redds," Kim shared, shaking her head in disbelief.

Mom smiled, and I felt my face going red.

"Jack, you should try finding him in some of these pictures," said Fly Bob.

I took the cue to get away and walked around to the different photos hanging in the restaurant. Soon, Mom joined me.

In these pictures, all sorts of people are holding salmon. Grandmas, old guys, even toddlers not able to lift the fish off the ground.

Then I spotted him - tall frame, brown hair, and unforgettable smile. It didn't matter that he was younger, it was Dad, those unmistakable green eyes - my eyes - looking back at me.

Kim was right. In the Polaroid picture he looks like me, only with a little more weight. His brown hair hangs under a Steelers hat. He was much skinnier as a kid, but still had an athletic build. Fly Bob stands next to Dad, only his beard is brown instead of gray, and he has less wrinkles. Still has that camouflage jacket though. They're both standing on the Russian River Ferry, smiling and holding up two salmon each.

I waved Mom over to the photo.

"Oh my goodness, Jack. There's your father. He looks so much like you." She put her arm around me and wiped some tears away with her shirt.

Next to that one, in another picture with Dad, I recognized a younger version of Ace with Fly Bob and even a teenage Kim. They were all lined up along the river holding their fishing rods high in the air. Under the picture, handwritten in loopy black letters, it said: "The Kenai Kids." They all look happy.

I pointed to Dad, and Mom ran her hand over his face.

It's really strange to have Dad's pictures hanging around the place, and the more I look around, the more I found Dad in other pictures.

A little too much to take in all at once, I think Mom quietly agreed because she let out a deep breath and went back to the booth.

Our food was waiting there, and Fly Bob was already chowing down.

"So I have to meet some fishing clients over on the Russian River today to give them some flies," Fly Bob shared between mouthfuls. "You're welcome to come over with me on the ferry and check out the neighborhood. I know the captain, so I can sneak you on. There'll be a lot of fishermen today going after the first run of reds, so I think the bears will stay at bay. It should be safe to take the trail."

"That sounds great, Bob," Mom said. "Thanks. Redds wanted us to experience the ferry. I'm looking forward to seeing what it's like, and so is Jack."

I recalled Dad mentioning it was an Alaskan tradition to take the Russian River Ferry across when we got to Cooper Landing. Just like our family tradition of walking across the Roberto Clemente Bridge before the baseball games to see the Pirates, I imagined a big Pittsburgh tug chugging along on the river.

After breakfast, we hop into the front cabin of Fly Bob's pick-up truck, a rusted light blue Ford Ranger. The R on the lift gate is rusted off so only ANGER is showing.

I speculated this was symbolic.

He has so much fishing equipment in the bed I wonder how it doesn't fall out, and when Salmo jumped into the empty space next to some wading boots. It seemed clear she'd done this before.

Fly Bob tried to make some small talk saying, "Jack, maybe tonight we can tie up some flies?" But I cut the conversation short with a quick, "Yep, maybe."

Mom kept it going, though.

"So Bob, do you sell a lot of your fly patterns?"

"Yeah, I spend most of my winters tying all the patterns I'll need for the summers. A lot of guys ask me ahead of time to tie up their favorite flies, and I make a few bucks. It's a modest living but it supplements my fishing habit." Fly Bob chuckled.

After a few miles ride to the ferry, we stepped out along the river, and I noticed the words "Russian River Ferry" painted in black along a green flat-bottomed boat about the size of two trucks. It was tethered from above to two cables which connected the shores on each side. The ferry had two benches along the railing which probably sat about twenty people.

Really, this is the ferry we've all been waiting for?

One at a time, we stepped onto the boat. I tried to keep my balance as it swayed with every step.

A kid with a Hello name tag with 'Captain' written underneath handed me a bright orange life jacket. I'm the only one he hands one to, and he says, "Take it...it's for the kids." He doesn't seem any older than me and wasn't even wearing one.

We all took a seat with plenty of legroom since we're the only passengers traveling over. I felt like the only idiot wearing a life jacket. Mom puts one on too to make me feel better. I was just wondering where the engine was hidden when the captain unties the rope from the shore and grabs the steering wheel.

He yells, "Hold on!"

Suddenly, the river whips the boat around and starts to pull us across. As the captain pointed the ferry diagonally upriver, the boat moved through the current faster than I expected. Then I realized – there were no engines on this baby.

I thought back to times when horses and wagons had to cross a river. If this was here back then, it must've been scary to bring them all along on such a tiny barge. We're only bringing some fishing gear and lunch, not our whole house. Still, it felt a little shaky putting our lives in the hands of a kid-captain and a flat-bottomed barge boat.

Even though the boat is named the 'Russian River Ferry,' we weren't crossing the Russian River. Fly Bob pointed out the spot above the Russian where the crystal-clear water mixed with the greenish gray of the Kenai.

"The glacial silt is what murks up the Kenai River," Fly Bob announced to no one in particular. "We're headed upstream to the gin-clear Russian."

The Kenai River powerfully swings us across the river by its downstream current. Because I couldn't see down to the bottom and wondered how deep it was, I stupidly asked the 'Captain.'

He replied, "Jump in and see."

Real funny. I'm sure he's told that one before.

We approached the other side within a few minutes, and I could see a group of anglers lined up like dominoes. They reminded me of opening day of trout fishing in PA.

"All these anglers are going after the Sockeye salmon," Fly Bob shared. "But we'll save the salmon fishing for another day."

We reached the dock in minutes, and the captain tied both pulleys to the pier. I saw a sign which read: *"Do Not Stand On The Dock Too Long."* I pondered the weirdness of the message but didn't bother asking the captain this time.

We all stepped off, and Fly Bob led the way upstream toward where the Russian River blends into the silty Kenai. The ferry spun about and made the return trip taking some fishermen to the other side.

As Fly Bob made his way upstream, he seemed like a rock star. Everyone knew him and waved like he was the King on the Homecoming court.

He hiked us to a place they call the 'Sanctuary,' where the clear waters of the Russian River mix with the murky Kenai to create a turquoise milkshake. It was off-limits to fish, though, because it was early in the salmon run, but he said they'll probably open it up soon after they start making their nests to spawn.

I turned a few rocks over to see the local bug life and discovered some of the same insect life we have back in Pennsylvania.

"It's amazing, isn't it, Jack?" Mom gazed at the scenery.

I had to admit, the mountains, the churning water, the wildlife – it was a lot to take all in.

"Yeah, I see now why Dad loved this place so much." I relented.

I watched as Fly Bob met his clients at the Sanctuary and made the fly-for-cash trade, like some kind of Alaskan spies trading information.

As we walked back downstream to the ferry, more and more anglers asked Fly Bob to share his flies.

The Russian River Ferry makes its way back across the stream to pick us up. This time we're joined by a lot more anglers all holding their stringers filled with their three-fish limit of bloody salmon. The power of the Kenai River to move the ferry back and forth was impressive, unlike any river Dad and I had ever fished together.

Once back on board, the Captain took us back across the Kenai. This time, I didn't ask any questions, and he didn't make me put on the stupid life jacket.

That evening, Mom convinced me to go check out Fly Bob's trailer home while she worked on Dad's book. I was exhausted and didn't want to walk over, but I didn't put up a fight.

The harsh Alaskan winters had been tough on Bob's trailer, and the silver finish that once decorated the outside had now peeled and rusted.

Pieced together like a suit of armor, the silver sheet metal encasing the trailer made it resemble a giant steel salmon. The letters *SILVER STREAM* had faded away where they once had been, leaving a rusted outline behind. An old '72 Pennsylvania license plate hung from its back bumper. The trailer blended in with the grasses, bushes, trees, and surrounding mountains as if it had been there for a thousand years.

Fly Bob didn't tend to his living quarters much either. I ducked through his oval door like Gandalf the Wizard walking into a hobbit's house. In the one-room house/trailer was a small rusty sink, a bunk bed, and a tiny desk. Stacks of plastic bins and containers were piled throughout the trailer with labels and markings on each one.

"So you think this is messy, eh?"

I shrugged my shoulders as I scanned the room.

"Well, I only come here to sleep and tie flies. I got it all organized in my own system."

"It's cozy," I said, maybe because it reminded me of my own bedroom mess at home. Salmo owned a padded bed next to Fly Bob's, and she didn't seem to mind the clutter. Salmo circled around and around in her bed, then cuddled up tightly into a ball, like a cat.

Flies were everywhere, hanging from the shelves, the walls; there was even a lamp with flies dangling around its shade. Like a science laboratory cooking up secret formulas, each row of bins had feathers, hooks, and countless tying materials.

"What was your father tying up before he died?"

Whoa, a little soon for that kind of question.

I still answered courteously, "Mostly nymphs and some dries once in a while."

"Well, this is my tying station." He sat down on a fold out chair by a small desk. "Want to tie one up?"

I shrugged my shoulders.

Without waiting for my reply, Fly Bob sat down at his tying station and tightened the large silver salmon hook already in the vise. It was about five times larger than the hooks Dad and I tied with.

"This is called the Krystal Woolly Bugger."

Bob trimmed the materials for the fly and arranged them on the table. Hen feathers, Chenille, Marabou feathers, and Krystal Flash. I recognized all the materials since we used them in our fly patterns. Some were natural materials found from the animals Dad hunted like feathers from Mallard ducks and pheasants or fur from White-tailed deer. There were also other synthetic materials used by fly tiers in their patterns.

Fly Bob wrapped the thread bobbin around the hook with precise turns to put the thread into place.

"So you got the Alaskan journal, eh?" Fly Bob asked.

"Yep."

"An Alaskan kid your age that grew up not far from here actually designed our flag – Benny Benson. You'll have to look up his story sometime. Pretty interesting."

OK, enough of the small talk. It was time. I breathed in deeply and asked the question that had been on my mind a long time.

"So why haven't I ever met you?"

A long pause filled the trailer.

"It's stupid grown-up stuff, that's all you need to know."

I couldn't let him off the hook.

"Why didn't you come to Dad's funeral?"

Fly Bob grunted. "We can talk about this some other time. Let's just tie." He avoided my questions.

Bob placed the marabou feathers on the hook and tied in the tail in silence.

But I couldn't let it go. "I called you 'No Fly Bob' before we left," I challenged.

Fly Bob shook his head and tied in the feathers and chenille of the Woolly Bugger at the bend of the hook. "I guess you got a point there," he said.

"You really afraid of flying?" I kept the questions coming.

"Haven't been on a plane in over thirty years."

Bob coiled the chenille down the hook shank to make the body of the fly, tied it off, and then he wrapped the saddle hackle feathers in tight turns toward the eye of the hook.

"Your father gave me a call a couple of months before he died. He worked so hard on the Alaskan guide book; he reached out to me since he saved the Kenai Peninsula piece for last. We decided it was a good time to finally mend the fences."

There were those fences again.

He finished off the fly by knotting it with a fancy looking whip finisher.

"This fly used to be one of his favorites to tie," Bob said, handing it to me. I saw him wipe his tears away on his shirt sleeve, but I didn't say anything. I didn't realize he'd get so emotional on me.

"Hold this," Bob commanded, as he fumbled through some fishing equipment till he found what he was looking for. He finally revealed a long object wrapped in what looked like old t-shirts.

"This is your father's old fly rod. Still good as new. I kept it all these years."

The rod was a nine weight, two piece, ten-foot fly rod with a purplish tint to it, though it changed colors from light to dark as Bob moved it in the trailer's dim light.

"Here, he'd want you to have it."

I held the cork handle and flexed the rod. Stronger and heavier than most of my rods, it bowed in my hands.

"Maybe we'll take that rod out and catch some fish sometime?"

"Maybe."

Maybe more questions need some answers, Old Man.

"Well, time to hit the hay. We all need some shut-eye." He mumbled and coughed. I inferred the tying session was over.

Apparently, I needed some Alaskan shut-eye.

We walked in awkward silence over to the cabin. Though it was late in the evening, the sun mocked me from well above the horizon, as if to remind me that I won't get a good night sleep.

As we came through the door, Mom peered up over piles and piles of the Alaskan Guide manuscript scattered on the cabin floor.

"Well, you're back. Any fishing plans yet?"

"Nope, just tied some flies." Bob spoke up before I did.

I gave Mom a hug and hurried up the ladder to the loft.

"Night, night, Jack-O," she called.

I laid Dad's rod next to the bed and set the Woolly Bugger on my hat.

The four-hour time difference still messed with my body, and even with the lights on downstairs and Mom and Fly Bob talking, I couldn't fight my heavy eyelids and fell asleep.

Suddenly, I stepped off the train car with no one in sight. I walked toward the gray glacial water beside the tracks. The silty liquid rushed by my feet when I reached the water's edge. The sun sparkled on the water as I noticed large silver shadowy shapes moving back and forth within the depths. Desiring to move across the water, I took the first step into the icy river. My right foot landed on top of a silver object. Then I took another step and another.

Using the silver stepping stones, I made my way into the middle of the rushing glacial water. The flashy shapes kept me safely afloat and were in-sync with my every movement. They worked as one to steer me through the rough currents.

Through the fog that had descended and hung atop the water, I spied a bulky shadow fly-fishing on the other side of the bank. Like a bear, I turned my head from side to side and up and down. I recognized that familiar pipe smoke scent.

I strode closer to the other side, and my father materialized more clearly through the fog. I relished seeing him in the water again, casting back and forth, and I matched my breath to the motion of his fly line.

Back and forth, back and forth.

My chest rose up and down. Moving closer, I picked up the pace and stepped quickly upon the silver shapes. The sky darkened as the clouds shadowed behind me. I sprinted. I was just a few feet from Dad.

Just a bit further.

Taking a lunge, I stumbled. The shapes below darted upstream all in one motion and left me. I splashed into the rushing currents and fought to stay above water, but the water was too cold and too strong. I sank into the murky depths, tangled in the watery blackness pulling me further downstream until I could no longer breathe.

Grasping for one last breath, I awoke.

Ugh, just a dream.

Was that how Dad felt when he was drowning? I couldn't bear to think about it.

Untangling the sleeping bag from around my body, I paused and gained my breath.

Something stuck out from under my sleeping bag.

Dad's rod.

Closing my eyes in the semi-darkness, I tried with all my might to fall back asleep.

Please!

Just one more chance to walk on the silver shapes and see Dad again.

How could I lose him to the water again?

I grasped the rod as my chest tightened enough to burst. I sat up, clutched the rod with both hands, and...CRACK!

I broke Dad's rod into pieces.

CHAPTER 5

July 7th - 7:27 a.m.

Dear Dad,

I'm so sorry.

I broke your rod. It was an accident···sort of.

I almost convinced myself that I broke the rod "accidentally."

I stopped writing mid-sentence and set the pencil down. I couldn't lie to Dad, and maybe Fly Bob may never speak to me again.

I curled back into bed and wanted to disappear like those silvery shapes in my dream. Mom was up already and cooking bacon and pancakes, her specialty even with limited supplies in the kitchen.

"Breakfast is ready, Jack-o-lantern," she called.

For a minute, I remained as motionless as the train from my dream, but then I rolled slowly out of bed and crawled down the ladder into the syrupy smell. I barely lifted my head to acknowledge Mom and Fly Bob sitting at the table.

"Wow, someone looks like he woke up on the wrong side of the bed," Mom mused, ruffling my hair while I sat expressionless. "What's wrong, buddy?"

"I just miss Dad."

Mom hugged me. "If you need me to stay back today, I can reschedule the meeting with the guides."

"I can watch him today, Jill." Fly Bob suggested, like I was some little Alaskan rescue puppy he'd be watching.

"I'll be OK, Mom. Just a little jet-lagged." I fibbed.

Mom's meeting with local fishing guides was important for the book. Dad had added a section called "Guide Secrets," and the last one needed was for the Kenai Peninsula. She'd done footwork ahead of time and contacted some local guides to share their thoughts for the book. I didn't want to ruin the opportunity for her.

A horn beeped outside the cabin.

"OK, that's them. You guys are good with breakfast, right? Here's some money in case you need to get lunch or snacks. I'll see you later today, probably after three. I'll have my phone and may have reception if you need to send a message." She kissed me on the forehead and brushed out of the cabin, leaving Fly Bob, Salmo, and me in silence.

"Are you ready to take that rod out and give it a try?" Fly Bob asked.

I stalled a little. "Actually, think I'll just hang around the cabin and check out the restaurant gift shop."

"Are you sure? It's gonna be a banner day. Less anglers on the water. Besides, I told your mom I'd look out for you while she's working on the book."

Man, this guy is pushy.

"Nope, I can take care of myself," I insisted, chomping a piece of bacon.

Fly Bob stood there dumbfounded. Then he tightened up his wader belt.

"OK. Suit yourself, if you need me, you can call my cell or there's a map to the trail on the kitchen counter. I'll be down on the Russian River Trail. Watch out for the wildlife if you go out."

Salmo trailed happily along with Fly Bob.

After Bob left, I decided to try to fix Dad's rod and attempt this Alaska fishing thing on my own.

How hard could it be?

I didn't need someone telling me how to fish.

I headed over to the gas station across the street and picked up some Duct Tape, Pop Tarts, caribou jerky, a pop, and a dozen egg flies. One fly was called the "Dingleberry" and looked like three eggs wrapped with yarn around a hook. Seemed like an Alaskan fly that would work.

The guy at the fly shop said there was a little creek nearby called Quartz Creek that was rarely fished. He said some of the salmon may have moved up into it already. Sounded like a good plan to me, and I could avoid Fly Bob.

Back at the cabin, I carefully wrapped the rod's broken parts by cutting small strips of Duct Tape.

Good as new!

Then I grabbed my reel, backpack sling, Bob's map, and the gas station egg flies and headed out.

The weather was cloudy and, in the seventies, not too bad of a fishing day. The fish are always less spooky during cloudy days. I picked up my pace as I followed the road onto the trail leading to Quartz Creek.

The trail was tight, so it didn't seem like many people had traveled it recently. It reminded me of the dark fairytale forests that characters were always getting themselves tangled within. I finally made my way down to the water, and the woods opened a bit. I could throw a rock across the narrow creek, and I had to admit I was glad I didn't have to get in the water to fish it. A pod of fish held in the small stream, so I strung up my fly line through the rod guides and tied on one of the Dingleberries. Then I added some weight above my line and plunked a cast above the fish.

After a few drifts over the pod, I watched as the Dingleberry snagged right on the dorsal fin of a silver fish. When the fish felt the fly pressure on its back, it exploded upstream taking my fly line with it. I wasn't ready for the commotion, and the line caught itself on my reel, bending the rod down.

SNAAAAAAP! CRACK!

"Ahhhhh!" The rod cracked in all the same places I'd taped it. Plus, the fly broke off the end of my line. The fish tore upstream with the rest of the pod.

I sat down holding the pieces of Dad's rod in my hands again.

What a disaster.

Just then, I heard a different kind of cracking sound coming down the trail. It sounded like a T-Rex knocking down trees in Jurassic Park.

All the bird noise and background sounds disappeared.

I spotted the head of the moose first. Within about fifty feet of me across the stream, it didn't seem to be stopping and was headed straight at me. I noticed a smaller moose right behind it. From my Life Science class, I remembered my teacher, Mr. Deramo, discussing not to mess with a momma and her babies in the wild, since they were very protective. This could be trouble.

"Nice moose, nice moose." I held my hands out and tried to sooth the beast, but it kept tromping through the grass straight for me at an amazing speed. I grabbed all the rod parts, turned, and booked it down the path the other direction. The moose was gaining on me, as I could hear it grunting and snorting. I tripped over a hidden root and went tumbling off the trail into some weeds. The thorns scraped my face as I landed head over heels a little off the gravel path.

The mother moose wasn't stopping as she tore through the brush. It seemed whatever she was running from had her mad at me too. I got to my feet at the base of a solid tree and quickly shimmied up as far as I could, using my arms and legs to drag myself up the trunk. Clutching the tree and pressing my face against the moist bark, I waited.

The moose paused underneath me and snorted. Her baby ran under her belly to camouflage between her legs. My heart pounded like an Alaskan train engine, but I stayed frozen in place as long as I could, hugging the tree and listening to her heavy snorts below.

She made a 'gruff' and 'huff,' looked around, then lowered her hackles. As the hair around her neck returned to normal, the cow turned towards the trail again and began slowly walking away with her little one trotting behind. She had obviously calmed down and didn't see me as a threat to her little one anymore.

Close call.

Tasting a salty flavor in my mouth, I realized blood was dripping from my forehead down my cheeks. As my torn sweatshirt and blood-stained arms attested, I must have really scraped everything while tumbling off the trail. Something I never noticed when my adrenaline was pumping earlier. I waited several minutes longer just to be sure, clutching the tree trunk until I heard the birds chirping again. Finally, I shimmied back down to the ground. My fore arms and legs burned, and my hands prickled with pain from holding the tree so tightly.

My pounding heart rate also returned to a normal speed. With the adrenaline rush evaporated, I suddenly felt exhausted and weak.

Mom might kill me if she found me like this.

Great way to start fishing in Alaska, Cooper.

I hobbled back onto the trail and made it back into town.

A park ranger noticed me bloodied and limping. He pulled his truck around, rolled down the window.

"You OK, kid?" He asked.

I don't usually talk with a stranger, but under the circumstances, I figured he could at least get me back to the restaurant. The ranger parked his truck and walked me back. He kept asking me questions, which was annoying, but I figured it was only a tactic to keep me distracted and alert.

Luckily, Kim was there, and she told the ranger she'd help me get washed up and into some new clothes.

She applied ointment on my face, arms, and legs and barraged me with questions. "How could you go down that trail all by yourself? Where's Fly Bob? Where's your mom?"

Little did I know, the ranger had already figured out who I was and called Fly Bob on his own. Seemed like the word was out that his family was in town.

Next thing I knew, Fly Bob walked into the restaurant with a stern look on his face.

"What the heck were you thinking, Jack?" Fly Bob scolded after hearing my side story. "That moose could've stomped you good." His furrowed brow looked a little like Dad's when he was upset.

Not long after, Mom showed up, and the whole mess blew up in my scratched face again. More questions, more barraging, and lots of explaining.

"Jack, how could you do such a stupid thing? You could've gotten really hurt." Mom's hands trembled as she squeezed mine. I could see tears welling up in her eyes.

"Sorry Mom...I just wanted to take some time to myself."

Fly Bob sat in the booth staring off into space. He didn't have much to say as he eyed the broken pieces of the rod sprawled on the booth table.

Don't know why, but I confessed right there on the spot.

"I broke Dad's fly rod yesterday. I don't know why I did it. I guess I was mad at him for not being here with us."

I turned and looked at Fly Bob. "I'm really sorry."

Mom looked confused, but sat next to me. We hugged for a long time. This time, it didn't feel too long.

Salmo got impatient and nudged us with her nose.

"I've been procrastinating in doing this," Mom said as she pulled Dad's Wheatley fly box out of her backpack.

I remembered right away it held the rest of Dad's ashes. After Dad's service in April when we scattered his remains in his favorite creek, we'd put the rest of his ashes in this fly box to bring to Alaska. Mom had saved a small portion to bury where he'd been born. I didn't realize how much I'd been dreading the time when she would bring it up again on this trip until I felt my gut seize.

"Jack, maybe today might be the right time to do it?" She waited for my response, and I hesitantly nodded.

"Bob, do you have a suitable spot where we can bury the rest of Redd's ashes?"

Fly Bob paused and said, "Sure, I think I have a good idea of where we could go."

"OK then, why don't Jack and I head back to the cabin and meet you later this evening. We can have a little service for Redds, together." She took a deep breath and composed herself.

"I have to package some salmon, and I can meet you back here around 5:00 p.m. Hey Jack, bring the pieces of your Dad's rod, too."

Mom and I walked back to the cabin, her arm through mine, and we took a long nap together. We'd slept for two hours, and it was refreshing since I didn't have any dreams this time.

Walking out onto the porch, I noticed the temperature had dropped through the afternoon. I went back inside and threw on a t-shirt, thermal underwear, a long sleeve flannel shirt, jeans, two pairs of socks and hiking boots. I didn't know where we were going, but I wanted to be warm. When Mom came out bundled up as well, we left the cabin and strode into the brisk air.

Fly Bob stood outside of the restaurant lugging a small shovel.

No one said a word.

He led us through the original trail that I first started on toward Quartz Creek, then veered off. At first, it looked as though no path existed, but Fly Bob moved a few branches aside here and there, and it became clear he had taken this route many times before. The well-worn foot trail was only wide enough to fit one person at a time. It seemed a little safer, too, since we were all going this time.

Fly Bob was first, then me, then Mom. Salmo trotted behind sniffing every sign of wildlife. On the sides of the path, the trees and brush stood tall and thick, leaving no room to stray. After a brisk thirty-minute walk up and over the hills, we could hear rushing water surging in the distance. Soon, we overlooked a section of fast-moving currents and waterfalls below.

Fly Bob called over the rushing water. "Your father nicknamed this spot 'Chutes and Ladders' after the board game."

I remembered playing that game with Dad as a child. He always made noises as he moved the game pieces up and down the board that kept us laughing while we played.

Good memories.

Given the amount of water cascading through the series of waterfalls below, it seemed like a dangerous place to wade, let alone fish. Thoughts of Dad's death flooded my mind. Dad had always reminded me to wade carefully. "Never cross your feet and always keep yourself balanced," he preached.

After staring down at the wild waters for a while, I noticed a silver rocket jump and break the water's surface. On closer inspection, I recognized large iridescent salmon stacked side by side within the current using their tails to shoot out of the water and up over the falls. When another salmon leaped, I noticed hundreds of them swimming in the strong, cold currents.

"Magical...aren't they?" Bob pondered. "These salmon are coming up the stream to spawn. The water comes down the chutes, and the fish go up the ladders to lay their eggs." Fly Bob pointed upstream. "This was your father's favorite spot to fish when he was little."

I envisioned Dad at a young age with his rod, vest, and hat casting to salmon and having a grand time.

"If you look down in the calmer waters, you'll see the females digging their nests with their tails. The nests are called redds," Fly Bob continued. "The female salmon wait for the males to come to fertilize the eggs."

We watched closely overhead gazing into the glassiness of the river as a massive salmon used her tail fin to stir up the silt and pebbles from the stream bed to create her redd. She spun around many times to get the nest just right. A little crater underneath provided a perfect redd for her eggs.

"Your father was such a great fisherman. He used to know exactly where to find the fish and catch them before they made their nests, so we nicknamed him 'Redds.' That how everyone remembers him up here."

I thought back to Ace thinking I was Dad and how his nickname meant so much more now.

The three of us stood for a while in silence gazing at the beauty of the water, the salmon, and the scenery.

"Let's put this old rod to rest," Mom said, breaking the silence and picking up the pieces of Dad's fly rod. "I think your father would like it that way."

I guess I had to agree and nodded.

Fly Bob used the shovel to dig a shallow hole that overlooked the falls. I placed the fly rod pieces in the dirt. Then Mom pulled out the wooden fly box with Dad's remaining ashes inside, kissed it, and put it in with the rod. With everyone's help, we refilled the hole with soil.

Mom said a prayer of thanks and blessing to the life of John "Redds" Cooper. Her voice wavered. "He was a good father, husband, and son."

"...and one heck of a fly fisherman," Fly Bob whispered.

Mom continued. "Thank you, Lord, for blessing us with his presence."

"Amen," we all answered.

All was calm except for the water rushing below.

I looked up at the pinkish sky and considered, "Do you think they have streams up in heaven?"

"What do you think?" Mom asked.

"I think he's probably up there fishing somewhere." I answered, leaning into her warmth.

"Me too," she smiled. Then we walked down the trail toward the cabin with Salmo close behind.

Fly Bob stayed behind to pay his respects a little longer.

Turning back, I saw him bending down over the grave and wondered what he was thinking in that moment.

At least I have Mom.

He has no one.

July 7th — 7:12 p.m.

Dear Dad,

I didn't know you had another favorite fishing spot. We buried your rod there. So now you'll be able to visit your favorite Alaskan spot whenever you want.

Fly Bob's taking Mom and me out early tomorrow to fish. Fly Bob is weird and smells like fish. He told me to wear my Alaskan sneakers, whatever that means.

I hope you don't mind that I'm fishing without you. I figured since he is your dad, you wouldn't.

Still wearing your camo hat.

Love you.

CHAPTER 6

My alarm buzzed at 6:28 a.m.

Fly Bob wanted to be on water by then to get a good spot, but I stalled a bit. I hit the snooze more than a few times after looking down and seeing Mom sound asleep. She had not slept well since April, and neither had I. Lately, we used the "jet-lag" excuse.

I took my time getting on my fishing gear and waders.

After I woke Mom, we walked in our waders over to meet Fly Bob at his trailer. Salmo basked in the sun on the front porch of the trailer and noticed us with a slow-motion tail-wag. It picked up speed as I came closer.

"Sam, how you doin', girl?"

As I reached for the trailer door handle, I saw a scribbled note attached to the door: *Flies on the table. Bring Salmo. Meet at the trailhead 7 AM.*

I glanced down at my watch: 7:23 a.m.

Inside the trailer, Fly Bob had left us all kinds of flies: pinks, purples, fluorescents, and greens. Even though I didn't know the names of the flies, most of them resembled the minnow streamers I fished with back home.

I stuffed as many flies as I could into my fly box. Now familiar with Dad's vest, I memorized everything that was in it and put the fly boxes in their secret compartments.

With our map, Mom and I worked out the way to the trailhead of the

Russian River. Salmo trailed along happily.

At the trail, Fly Bob leaned against a sign:

> ### ALWAYS
> ### HAVE A BUDDY
> ### IN BEAR COUNTRY!

Pictured next to the words were two cartoon bears with their arms around each other.

Kind of creepy.

"Sorry we're late." Mom announced.

I would never be late fishing with Dad. We had a pact never to be late for church, sports, or fishing.

Fly Bob wrinkled his eyebrows again, reminding me of Grumpy, from the Seven Dwarves. He continued rigging up the fly rods without looking up.

"Hopefully, my favorite hole isn't taken already." With that, Fly Bob gruffly handed us each a rod and started down the Russian River trail making me feel like Dopey, lagging behind. I glanced at Mom and shrugged my shoulders as she raised her eyebrows. We hurried to catch up.

Man, this guy is serious about salmon.

As we entered the thicker wilderness, Fly Bob put up his hand and stopped as if he heard something. "Young fella, if you hear me whistle, I want your full attention. This is bear country, and the last thing we want is for the bear to see us before we see them. Be alert and have your 'bear sense' about you. Got it?"

I nodded even though I knew I didn't have any bear senses just yet. The gigantic pistol strapped to Fly Bob's wading belt eased my fears a little.

Fly Bob then hurried down the gravel trail. Along the path, I stuck out my arm and ran my hand through the large green moist leaves, only to discover thorns the size of nails.

"Ouch!" Underneath the large leaves of the plant hid spiny stems that cut into my hand.

Luckily, Mom had some tissues with her to stop the bleeding.

"Gotta stay out of that Devil's Club," Fly Bob barked, "That stuff will tear up your waders when you walk through it and put the pain on you." He showed us some scars on his forearms. "Got those getting away from a moose."

I could relate.

"My family used to hang a piece of devil's club over our doorway," Fly Bob shared. "They said it warded off evil."

The forest gave me an early warning, so I decided to stick to the path.

As we traveled a quarter mile further, Fly Bob stopped again beside two towering trees. Colored in a slate gray, they looked like marble columns reaching to the sky.

"Welcome to the gates of paradise," Fly Bob smiled. "These cottonwoods are the entrance to my Alaskan playground."

Mysteriously, the giant trees rose into the low hanging fog. I doubted I could even wrap my arms around the bases. I recognized the gray bark as a bigger version of the one I climbed yesterday during my moose incident. I snapped a quick picture as the fog covered the treetops which reached all the way into heaven.

Bob trekked forward again, and I hurried to keep pace. More than once, Fly Bob paused to check for signs of wildlife, and we almost bumped into him. Sometimes, I only heard the birds chirping and the sound of my own heartbeat while holding my breath. Even Salmo obeyed and knew when to stop and wait for Fly Bob to move forward.

"Ah, here's some proof." Bob picked up a broken mushroom that was in the middle of the trail, observing it closely. "Yep, I figured that mushroom was out of place. A young grizz must've taken a bite out of it and decided it wasn't a very good meal. There's been a young'un around these parts lately. Sometimes, they're the most curious. Let's keep our eyes and ears open."

Bear tracks came out of the woods and onto the trail where Bob found the mushroom. Mom placed her foot next to the paw print. It measured the length of her foot and a bit further. I pulled my camera out and took another pic. Maybe there was more out there in the woods than I could see.

We followed the trail for about a mile before Fly Bob stopped by a flowing spring.

"This is my water'n hole. Fill up your canteens here so we can prepare for the hike down to the river."

I wanted to ask how much longer but didn't want to seem like a wimp. He wasn't going to show me up on a fishing hike, so I kept quiet.

"Water's safe to drink here since it's filtered through the rock. This is always my halfway fill-up since we can't drink the water down below."

The coolness soothed my throat. Maybe this magical liquid could ward off any wild animal encounters? Salmo took her licks from the spring. She must have enjoyed the water from this spring many times before.

I glanced down at my feet and chuckled aloud.

"What's so funny?" Mom asked.

"I just figured out Alaskan sneakers are my wading boots."

"Yep, get used to them," Fly Bob said. "If the fishin's good, we might be staying in these waders until midnight!"

Wow, fishing until 12 a.m.! No wonder everybody in this town wears their waders everywhere.

"Only another half-mile to get to the river, but now we're going to hit some rough walkin' territory."

We turned off the gravel trail to a tighter path. The forest closed in as we hiked downward into the canyon. It became steeper and narrower, and we used tree roots and rocks to step our way down to the water. For what seemed like the length of a football field, I watched Fly Bob's steps as he carefully placed each foot on the rocks below. Mom and I followed in his footsteps, moving down closer to the river. As we gained ground, I could hear the faint sound of water rushing below.

"Keep your eyes open down here." Fly Bob ordered. "We're here, and so are the bears. Take your time and watch each step."

"Bob, what exactly do we do if we get close to a bear?" Mom innocently asked.

"Well, as I see it – bears react in four different ways. One, they quickly skedaddle. Two, they stay for a few minutes to check you out, and then they grunt and walk away. Three, they protect their spot, or four, they chase you. Let's just hope for the first two. We'll make enough noise, so they'll know we're coming."

Mom gulped and grimaced at me.

"Here, this might ease your fears a bit."

He handed us each a small little spray container of Bear Spray.

"Watch how you use this. It's a high dose of pepper spray. Keep it away from your face and always point it towards the bear if we have any confrontations."

"Will bear spray work?" I asked Fly Bob.

"Maybe, or it might just flavor you before they eat you." He cackled.

I took that as a 'no.'

"When will you use the pistol, Bob?" Mom read my mind, as I looked at Bob's holster.

"Well, with bear spray, you can sometimes protect yourself without killing the bear, but unfortunately, it's not always effective if they're intent on aggression or it's a sow with cubs. Once I pull out the pistol, I might have to put it down."

I hoped it wouldn't come down to that.

Fly Bob kept walking and grunted something about staying close, so we did.

We heard the river before we saw it. The power of crystal-clear water cascading through the valley generated a mighty sound. When we arrived at the water's edge, I was surprised to discover the great Russian River was smaller than I'd expected. I looked at it more carefully, though; it was clear it would present challenges and was too deep to wade all the way across. Giant boulders lined the river creating short pools that dropped from one into the next.

Fly Bob led us further downstream along a thin walking path that cut through heavy brush. Bob stopped to rig up his rod by a large flat boulder. "Beneath that lone spruce tree that overhangs the water is the best spot on this river," he said, pointing downstream. "And those darn boys got down here first!"

The canyon widened from a small waterfall to large runs and pools. That meant shallower water to wade.

I noticed a dead salmon laying on the edge of the water with only a head connected to the tail, its flesh eaten down to the white bones. I pulled out my phone to get a picture of the salmon carcass. After nudging it with my foot, the putrid salmon smell hit my nose.

What animal had been snacking on this salmon? It gave off a foul odor. Salmo didn't seem to mind as she walked over, sniffed at it, and moved on. Mom had a handkerchief around her neck and repositioned it up over her nose. I placed my rainbow trout buff over my nose like a western bank robber.

I spotted more salmon carcasses scattered all over the place. The rotting corpses reminded me of death.

Death is everywhere. Can't shake thoughts of Dad.

I didn't notice that Fly Bob had already waded out into the chilly water, but the water's edge stopped me in my tracks.

Fly Bob turned around, "Whaddya waitin' for? Come on in, the water's fine."

Never had I been scared of wading, but since Dad was taken by water, a new fear seemed to engulf me like a dark blanket.

Bob turned and waded further into the river, putting the water level up to his waist.

I froze.

Mom sensed my fear. "It's OK, Jack. You don't have to do it if you don't feel ready."

I didn't know if that comment was for me or for her.

It's now or never, Cooper. Don't be a wimp.

I forced my legs into the frigid water and followed Bob like an awkward duckling trailing its family.

"I'll be writing here near the shore if you need me," Mom assured. Salmo stayed back near the bank and sat with Mom.

Maybe they were the smart ones. I waded until the water reached my waist. Luckily, I was tall like Dad, but skinny enough for the water to rough me up a bit.

Fly Bob walked toward three anglers fishing by the spruce. One was a tall, lanky fisherman with a yellow ball cap. Another was a short, stout fellow who filled his waders completely and wore a raggedy cowboy hat. I recognized the third one upstream by her YETI hat and tie-dyed wolf hoodie.

"Well, look who finally showed up," shouted the tall guy with the yellow hat.

"Yeah, we already limited out today," the other one laughed.

"Right, right. I'm sure you didn't save any fish for us," Fly Bob replied.

"Who's the cheechako?"

"Who you callin' a cheechako? He's related to me, so he has fishin' blood in him." Fly Bob chortled.

I caught up and Fly Bob introduced me to his fellow Alaskan fly fishing guides.

"Jack, this is Hal, the *second-best* fishing guide in Alaska, and the other husky one is Buff, who just comes along to snag fish."

"Hey, who you callin' husky?" Buff grumbled.

"Guys, meet my grandson, Jack. He's going to catch his first salmon today. His mom, Jill, is over there on the shoreline," said Fly Bob, pointing at my mom who waved to the guys.

I shook Hal's hand, then Buff's.

"Good luck, man. We've been using these flesh flies and killing 'em all morning."

Fly Bob winked, "Don't believe a word they say. We've got the salmon magnets today."

He led me a little further downstream to respect the other anglers' room to fish. Bob scanned and squinted at the water.

"Gotta look for the windows, the slack water – where you can see the fish. You'll only catch glimpses of them. Maybe a tail or a shadow on the river gravel. Wait for the calmer water to pass by, and you can see down into the water column. I call 'em my fishin' windows."

From his angle, I tried to glimpse through the fishing windows, but didn't see anything.

"There! Two fish right there!" Fly Bob pointed to a section of water.

I nodded and pretended to see them. *Nothing.*

Even with my polarized sunglasses, I couldn't spot the fish that Fly Bob could see without glasses. The reflection and rocks camouflaged them just like they wanted.

Bob attached the hand tied Krystal Woolly Bugger to the end of his leader and added some split shot weight above it to reach the fish. Then, he expertly made a tight roll cast under a low hanging branch. I could tell, he had hit this spot before.

Bob worked the fly line so that his bugger would drift naturally with the water current.

ZZZZZZZZZzzzzzzzzzzzzzzzzzzz!

Fly Bob's reel screamed as the salmon snarfed up the fly on the first drift.

Amazing, they really were there!

"FISH ON!" Bob yelled.

A tinge of familiarity ran up my spine. It was like Dad himself had said it.

The silver flash zipped upstream, then down, then back up again. Salmo ran back and forth along the water's edge mimicking the fish's movements up and down the water.

Even though it seemed like chaos, Fly Bob calmly held his ground and watched as the fish tried to use the current to escape.

Bob grabbed my rod and handed his oversized rod to me. "Here you go, young man."

As I took the rod, I underestimated the tug and almost fell in the frigid water. The fish struggled against the force of the rod.

"If you fall in, keep your legs in front of you until you can get your footing to a shallower spot," Fly Bob advised.

Thanks for telling me that, now.

The salmon tore upstream a little into Buff's pool. The guides reeled their rods in so they wouldn't tangle. Hal tilted his rod into the water to spook the fish back to me.

I gained control and reeled the monster closer into shallow water where I could observe the enormous size of the fish and then brought him into shore. The fish rolled over a little, and Fly Bob waited with the net.

Bob pulled the salmon out. Even in Fly Bob's large grasp, the cradled salmon looked like a mammoth submarine, well around twenty inches.

I scanned the shore for Mom and saw her running all the way down the trail to see my catch.

"Meet your first red salmon," Fly Bob proclaimed.

The silvery-blue scales glistened in the sunlight.

"It's silver," I observed, "so why's it called a red?"

"You'll see when we catch one big enough to gut," Fly Bob responded as he carefully removed the bugger from the fish's jaw and put it in the net.

"Let's carry it over to your mom and get a picture of this guy."

We reached the bank, and he handed me the fish from the net. It sagged in my arms like a wet raincoat.

"Wow Jack, that's some fish," said Mom, her mouth agape.

Hal and Buff came over to congratulate me, even though I didn't actually hook it myself. Even the restaurant girl moved her way down to us.

"Time to Grip-n-Grin," Fly Bob said.

"Not a Cheech anymore," Buff shouted.

"Hold him under the belly and grasp his tail. Keep him close to the water." Fly Bob instructed.

Hal snapped a great picture on my phone of me holding the salmon with the snow-capped mountains behind. It was cool to hold my first salmon, and I wondered what Dad would be saying now.

"Ehhh, kinda small," the restaurant girl declared, shrugging her shoulders. She walked back to her spot upstream.

"Time to let 'em go," Bob said. "We call those little ones 'jacks' since they come back a little early from the ocean to spawn. So I guess we got a jack for Jack! But there's bigger ones than that to catch."

I placed the salmon back in the frigid water. Immediately, the red gathered up strength, surged its tail, and darted upstream. Salmo made a splash as if she would chase it but decided to stay by Fly Bob's side.

Hal patted me on the back. "Good job, I'm sure we'll be seeing a lot more of you on the water this summer. Nice to meet you as well, Jill."

Buff nodded too, and they left us standing in the shallows as they waded back upstream.

"Great job, young man." Fly Bob reached for my hand and held on. "Now you're ready."

"For what?" I questioned.

Fly Bob turned my hand over and pointed to it. "You're ready to catch the Salmon Slam."

"Start with your thumb." He made a thumbs-up sign. "Thumb rhymes with Chum. We call them Dog Fish."

Salmo licked her chops on cue as if Fly Bob had fed her a Chum before.

"Next you have your pointer." He squeezed my index finger. "This number one reminds you that the Sockeye Salmon are number one to eat. We call them Reds, since their flesh on the inside is a reddish color, and they're so delicious."

"The King Salmon is next," Fly Bob finally released my hand.

Man, he has a strong grip.

Fly Bob made a three with his thumb, pointer, and middle fingers. "The longest finger represents the daddy of all the Alaskan salmon, the King, or what the natives call the Chinook."

Pointing to my ring finger, Fly Bob continued, "Next are the Coho Salmon, or what we nickname the Silvers. Remember those on your fourth finger since married couples keep their rings on this finger. They really will give you a fight on a fly rod. They're the acrobats of the salmon."

"Last, on your pinkie," Bob dangled his pinkie finger in the air, "is the Pink Salmon. We also call them Humpies, since they develop a hump on their backs during spawning season. The pinks make a run only on the even years, and this summer's one of them. So, there you have it – all five species of Alaskan salmon to remember on one hand."

"That would be great to add to Dad's book." Mom added.

We quizzed one other on each species.

"Good job," Fly Bob affirmed. "If you have any luck, you'll be able to catch the Grand Slam of Salmon – all five species in one summer! Only then will you be a true Alaskan fly fisherman. It's not easy. Mother Nature staggers the salmon runs at different times during the season so they all have a chance to spawn and reproduce. Got to hit it at the right time. You can be the best fisherman in the world, but if the fish aren't here, you gotta look for them somewhere else."

Dad's voice rang in my ears. *"Part of being a good fisherman is being at the right place at the right time."*

"Your dad spent a few summers trying to catch the Slam..." Bob looked off over the mountain range as if he were trying to recall a memory.

"And he never did it?" Mom asked.

"Nope, Redds never was able to catch the whole Salmon Slam. Never was here long enough to get 'em all in one summer. He loved fishing for salmon, though. He was a great fisherman, wasn't he? Looks like you have the Cooper fishing blood in you, Jack. Only four more, and you'll do it. You might be able to find them all this summer."

It sounded like a daunting task.

"Let's catch our limit and get some bigger bucks to cook up tonight. Gotta get them while the gettin's good," Fly Bob chortled.

He shuffled over to the fishing hole and cast again. I followed him over, took a few steps downstream, and made a few casts on my own, but I couldn't get anything.

At one point, Hal, Buff, Fly Bob, and the restaurant girl all had reds on their lines. At this rate, they all would catch and keep their limits of three fish per day pretty quickly. They made it look so simple.

Meanwhile, I couldn't even hook one. It was very frustrating, especially since I was usually the one with a bend in my rod.

After twenty minutes, I still hadn't had a nibble.

What was I missing?

I tried to concentrate on my drift, adjusting my feet just a little forward before making another cast. Immediately, my line went tight, and I was into one. The silver flash sped upstream so fast that Fly Bob couldn't even get his rod out of the way. My fly reel spun out of control.

The power of this fish shocked me and came right through the rod. I didn't even notice Fly Bob shouting things like, "Work him down stream" and "Curve your rod." Eventually, I gained some control of the fish and worked him through the currents. When the fish tired, I led the red to Fly Bob's awaiting net, and he scooped it up like a pro.

"Great job, young man!" He congratulated me. It felt better this time since I caught it myself. Mom waded out to us, too.

Fly Bob removed the fly from the fish's curved jaw. This Sockeye looked fierce.

"Let's get a pic of this guy and put 'em on the stringer."

The silvery salmon sagged in my arms as Fly Bob snapped a photo on my phone. Mom put her arm around me and got in the picture.

Believe it or not, I caught two right after that the same way and 'limited out' with three on the stringer. I could continue to fish, but I couldn't keep any more.

I took a break and sat with Mom on a shallow gravel bar facing upstream while she read a book. The water rushed along the tops of our boots. From a distance, I studied the fluidity of Fly Bob's casts. Even though it was different from fishing back home, it felt like I was fishing with Dad.

We'd fish together for a while, and then fish alone a little. After an hour, we'd always meet back up and share which flies were working and how the water conditions were. I loved sitting and watching Dad fish.

I miss him.

I took a deep breath and held it for a while.

Surrounded by the beauty of the landscape, I looked down and noticed the smallest of details: my pointer finger rested on the cork handle of the fly rod.

The number one fish is the Sockeye.

I exhaled.

The first fish.

"Mom, I think I have something I could do for Dad."

I would do something for him that he'd never been able to do.

I would catch the *Grand Salmon Slam* – all five species of salmon in one summer.

CHAPTER 7

ALASKAN ☆
FACTS:

☆ ☆
☆ ☆
☆ ☆
☆ ☆

'Cheechako' means a newcomer.
'Sourdough' means a person who lived
through at least one Alaskan winter.

July 9th — 9:14 a.m.

Dear Dad,

You would be proud. I caught my first salmon yesterday on a Krystal Woolly Bugger and a bunch more after that.

I could barely hold onto the rod when I hooked one. I caught this one buck, a male, that was gigantic! He gave me a real hard fight. We kept three big ones each for dinner - that was our limit for the day. Then we let the rest go. I lost count how many we caught.

Fly Bob filleted the reds up. It was cool to see the bright red inside — he was right. He cut four fillets out of each fish and said he would cook up some fresh salmon on the grill, Yum! Even Salmo enjoyed some of it.

Well, I'm going to try to catch the Salmon Slam this summer — for you. One down and four to go. Bob says the chums are running up the Funny River soon, if that's a real river. Now I'm beginning to understand why you wanted to go after these guys.

I walked over to the Lodge for breakfast in the morning since Mom was already there, but I was focused on more important things than socializing. With the daunting task of catching the slam, I really wanted to go someplace where I could learn about salmon up close, like a salmon hatchery.

Right away, I spotted the restaurant girl sitting in her same booth. I didn't see Mom, so I sat down at an opposite booth and pretended to read the placemats. After a few minutes, the girl walked over and sat down in the seat across from me. This time, she had her hair up in a ponytail without a hat. Her wolf hoodie looked like she'd worn it all summer, but she had some shorts on this time. I tried not to notice.

"So you finally caught a red, eh?"

"Uh, yah. Finally got the hang of it."

"You're lucky Fly Bob's your grandpa."

"Um, I guess."

Didn't know how to respond to that one.

"Did you get any good ones?" She asked.

"Yeah, I caught a few more on my own that were bigger."

"You have a name? My name's Junior."

I swallowed the lump in my throat. "I'm Jack...from Pittsburgh."

Ugh, I gotta stop doing that.

"OK, Pittsburgh. Maybe I'll see you around on the river."

With that, Junior headed back to the kitchen, and I finally exhaled.

Fly Bob soon walked out of the kitchen with Mom carrying steaming omelets. He set one down in front of me.

"Try this, I call 'em my Salmon Specials," Fly Bob said. The eggs had little flakes of salmon in them. I knew Dad would scarf these up.

"Who was the girl?" Mom pried with a curious smile.

"Um, nobody, she just lives here." I blushed. Mom can read me like a book.

Fly Bob chimed in. "That's Junior. Her mom is Kim, the waitress."

I changed the subject. "Dad listed a salmon hatchery nearby in his itinerary. Can we go there today, Mom?"

"Wish we could. Bob, how can we get there?"

"Well, I'd love to take you guys, but I have some last-minute fishing clients to take out today. It's too bad your mom can't drive a shift stick, or I'd give you 'Ole Blue' for the day since I'm not using it."

"Are you kidding? I used to drive my dad's Chevy Bronco to take Redds fishing in the backwoods all the time. See what you've missed, Bob!"

Good one, Mom.

"OK then, that settles it." Bob tossed the keys to Mom. "Blue's a little finicky, but she will do the job. If you take the Sterling Highway toward Soldotna, there's a salmon hatchery down along the coast about fifteen miles. You can't miss it. Have a good day, and tell the salmon to head further up the river so I can catch 'em!"

Mom drove Fly Bob's 'Ole Blue' like a champ. The highway played tag with the Kenai River all the way as it curved and crossed the river over and over. Every time we drove over a bridge, I peeked out the window like Salmo to see if anyone was fishing.

Fly Bob was right, you couldn't miss the hatchery. We noticed the concrete holding tanks zigzagging their way from the coastline up into the fish hatchery building. The intense smell slapped at my nose the second I stepped out of the truck. There were a lot of tourists taking pictures and viewing the salmon holding tanks.

Luckily, it was open to the public today.

"Ew, it smells like Fly Bob's jacket out here!" Mom kidded as she wrinkled her nose.

Hundreds of dorsal fins lined their way up the concrete enclosures. I blinked my eyes as if I didn't believe it. Salmon stacked themselves from caudal fin to head, and they swam and hopped together up the aptly named fish ladder.

Mom spotted a large wooden sign in the shape of a salmon. "Jack, look at this. It says that after hatching here and heading out to the ocean, these salmon find their way back to this exact location to spawn."

We walked uphill along the fish ladders and continued to read the salmon signs which led us up to the last enclosure. All the salmon had congregated there. The fish ladder simulated a realistic river where the salmon had to move from enclosure to enclosure by jumping out of the water or making their way through a complex series of seven tunnels to reach the top.

A fish chart hung along the tank enclosures. It had exactly what I was looking for in my quest for salmon. The chart displayed the runs of each salmon species. Especially important for me were the limited ranges of time each kind of fish was available or best time to catch them.

"OK, Mom," I said. "I've already caught the Red. Now to catch the slam I have to catch a King, a Pink, a Chum, and a Silver...uh oh, that one might be a problem."

FISH AVAILABILITY CHART					A – Fish Available		P – Peak Fishing					
	Jan	Feb	Mar	Apr	May	Jun	Jul	Aug	Sep	Oct	Nov	Dec
King Salmon (Chinook)					A	P	P	A				
Sockeye Salmon (Red)					A	P	P	A	A			
Pink Salmon (Humpy)						A	P	P	A	A		
Chum Salmon (Dog)					A	A	P	P	A	A		
Coho Salmon (Silver)							A	P	P	A		

All but the Silver Salmon were in peak fishing in July. We were scheduled to fly out in early August, but that couldn't worry me just yet. The Silvers still seemed available this summer.

In the last enclosure, hundreds of salmon swam aimlessly around the tank in just a few feet of water. The fish were stacked so close that I couldn't drop a rock to the bottom. One of the fish biologists walked through waist high water in knee-high waders pushing the fish and holding a large net. Then he picked out a particularly large salmon and scooped him from the others.

"What kind of salmon is that?" A passerby asked.

"That's one of our Kings. You can pick 'em out since they're a lot bigger than the Chums. They also have the black gum line."

The King splashed around until it settled in the net. This prehistoric salmon wasn't like the small brook trout that inhabited our secret stream in Pennsylvania. Its blue green back glistened in the sun. It had black spots on some of its body and on the tail. The King opened its mouth and showed off its dark gums. This thing would be massive, especially to catch on a fly rod.

The man moved it out of the holding station and into a running channel marked for the Kings. They separated the species that ended up here by hand and net.

Inside the hatchery doors, we walked toward the enormous aquarium tanks. Mom put a few bucks in the donation box hanging on the left to help fund the salmon hatchery. The halls were lined with aquariums filled with Alaskan sea life. One tank caught my attention. Labeled 'Salmon Eggs,' it held the actual eggs of a salmon. I pressed my forehead up against the tank. The pinkish/orange round eggs glowed with two small dots as eyes inside. Hundreds, maybe thousands of them, the size of a pencil eraser, stacked up in a small gravel redd like Fly Bob showed us at the Chutes and Ladder hole. This was it – the beginning of life for these salmon. Hatching in freshwater and then making their way out to the ocean when they were strong enough to handle swimming in the currents.

Wonder how many of these little guys will survive?

Further down the hallway were alevins, fry, and fingerling tanks - the entire salmon life cycle. I recognized it as very similar to the trout life stages, although trout didn't have to survive out in the saltwater.

"Hey Jack, check this out," Mom called.

I walked over to a display with my name 'JACK' in big red letters. I read it out loud:

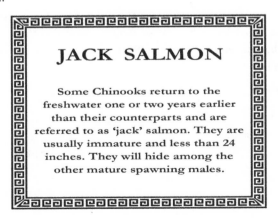

JACK SALMON

Some Chinooks return to the freshwater one or two years earlier than their counterparts and are referred to as 'jack' salmon. They are usually immature and less than 24 inches. They will hide among the other mature spawning males.

Fly Bob was right about the jack salmon.

"I'm not immature, am I?" I asked Mom jokingly.

Her eyes widened, eyebrows went up, and she gave me a shrug of the shoulders.

I guess I deserved that.

We continued to the end of the hallway, and I noticed a familiar sight. The Alaskan Flag was displayed on the wall along with a picture of a seventh grader named Benny Benson, the flag designer kid that Fly Bob mentioned.

I walked closer and studied the picture of Benny holding his version of the flag with blue silk and seven gold stars to represent the Big Dipper and one for the North Star.

The display had Benny's own description of his winning flag design in 1927, *"The blue field is for the Alaska sky and the Forget-Me-Not, an Alaskan flower. The dipper is for the Great Bear – symbolizing strength. The North Star is for the future of the state of Alaska, the most northerly in the Union."*

I remembered studying the constellations in science class. The Big Dipper also known as Ursa Major the Big Bear was one of my favorites since it was easy to recognize, and I could see it from my backyard. Dad enjoyed pointing out the constellations and stories behind them. I think I remember him mentioning something about the bear symbolizing strength. I wished I'd paid more attention to his star stories when he was alive.

Turns out, Benny had a tough childhood, too. He lost his mom to pneumonia when he was three, his house burned down, and then he was sent to an orphanage. He said the reason he wanted to enter the contest was to honor his family, be strong, and to make things right for Alaska. The last line shared what Alaskans thought of Benny's new flag design: "Alaskan Natives, who had struggled with their own stories of tragedy and loss, saw in Benny and his flag symbols of enduring strength."

Mom joined me at the display and quietly read.

I expected her to comment on something about my journal and having strength through tough times and honoring your family, but she just smiled and held my hand. Sometimes moms know just what's needed.

On our way out of the hatchery, a crowd of people huddled along the ladder taking pictures and video while 'ohhing and ahhing.' Sure enough, some grizzly bears had made their way to the river entrance of the fish ladder below and were pawing at the salmon swimming by. I joined the tourists and got some great bear video on my phone.

I don't know about all the fuss Fly Bob makes about bears. Seemed like they're harmless enough today. We made the drive back to our cabin, and Mom stopped for a coffee at a stand along the way. I pulled out my journal to write:

July 9th — 4:19 p.m.

Hi Dad,

If I can get a chum pretty quick, I figure then it's onto getting that King salmon. Fly Bob said there's a chance for the chums and maybe even kings to be in the Funny River tomorrow, so we're going fishing for the rainbows that eat the salmon eggs and the chums. From the pictures in the restaurant, there are some monster rainbows there, too.

I.) CHUM

II.) ~~RED~~

III.) KING

IV.) SILVER

V.) PINK

I listed the five salmon on the inside back cover of my journal in the order of my hand using Roman Numerals. Dad loved using Roman Numerals since the NFL used them for each Super Bowl. He had a baseball hat in his den that had the Steelers' six wins on it: IX, X, XIII, XIV, XL, XLIII. He'd quiz me on the numbers up to one hundred. Just another little reminder of what I loved about Dad.

I crossed off the first one I caught, the Red.

Closing it, I stared at the front cover for a while.

Some stars in a pattern on a blue background. What a simple design for such a complex kid. I thought of Benny and felt sorry for him.

How could a kid be so positive about a flag when all this bad stuff happened to him?

Guess he had to 'be tough' too.

CHAPTER 8

Fly Bob came over to the cabin and woke me up this time in the early morning. We headed down the Sterling Highway in 'Ole Blue' again towards Soldotna to the Funny River. I fought to keep my eyelids open during the twenty-minute ride.

I woke up inside the parked truck, and Fly Bob was gone. Looking out of the misty window, I barely made out a smaller stream with fog rising from it. Fly Bob was knee deep, casting through the mist, or as Dad would say, he was *"working the water."* Maybe the fish wouldn't be feeding yet, but I guess Fly Bob knows better than me.

The stretch was a long flat of water that led into a fast run of riffles. It had to be only three to four feet deep since Fly Bob's waders were mostly dry.

That's good – shallow wading water.

I stepped out of the truck and quickly put on my waders and boots. The clouds spurted a little spray in the chilly temperature, but I soon warmed up inside my Alaskan sneakers.

As I scanned the water, I spotted hundreds of shadows through the crystal-clear water. This warmed me up even more. The chums swam their way up the river like greyhound dogs jockeying for positions. Funny that he'd called them chum dogs when he talked about them before. Fly Bob held up his "chum thumb" and motioned me to wade carefully.

I stopped in my tracks and watched as Bob drifted a fly across the pool right over the fish. It seemed he was sight casting to a particular chum salmon. As Bob's fly dropped just below the water's surface and swung in the current, one fish took a swipe at it and missed. Another one, whacked after it.

The salmon behind it licked the fly in, and Fly Bob raised his rod tip with ease.

ZZZZZZZZZZZZZZZZzzzzzzzzzzzzzzzzzzz!

Fly Bob's reel whizzed.

"Guess he was ready for that Everglow!" Fly Bob chuckled. "These fish love those glow-in-the-dark flies. I knew they'd be working this morning. Glad I tied some up last night!"

The fish tore through the pool but didn't have enough room to move. So it did a few convulsions and grew tired.

Fly Bob soon led the catch to his side. I quickly recognized by its hooked jaw and the purplish-green colorations along its body that this salmon was indeed a chum. Since I decided to catch the slam, I'd been reading up on all the salmon types.

Bob worked the feisty fish into his wet hands.

"See these teeth?" Fly Bob pointed to the fish jaw as he removed the fluorescent green fly from its mouth. "Now those are some choppers, eh? They will get even bigger when it spawns out."

This dog looked ferocious.

Fly Bob then placed the chum back into the frigid water. "Let's get a fresher one to keep. They're much better to eat that way." The fish forged forward and began to swim upstream.

"OK Jack, ready to catch one?"

Fly Bob handed me his rod. "I only let a certain few have the privilege of using this one. I call it the Excalibur." Special wooden trim encircled the cork handle which was encrusted with a turquoise-colored stone.

"That's 100 percent Alaskan jade in the handle. I carved it down to use in the rod along with the cork handle. I crafted this whole rod a while back. Wrapped the ferrules myself."

Fly Bob had tied the rod ends with little colorful feather markers so that when you matched up the ends of the rod pieces, they pointed to each other. The cork handle had various colors of cork stacked together to give it a unique design. The rod was a piece of artwork.

"Just drift with the current and try to swing that Everglow through the water. Hopefully, the chums will take a chomp at it."

OK, this should be like swinging a wet fly at home.

Dad showed me the technique of putting a belly in my fly line and allowing the current to pull the fly downstream at just the right speed. This gives the fly a little movement like a creature trying to get away.

I allowed my fly line to belly in the current. I could tell Fly Bob was a little impressed with my line technique.

With the first swing, I pulled the fly line in too fast and made the fly move too swiftly in the current. I stripped in the line and made a second cast.

On the second swing, a large bulldog of a fish followed the fly downstream about twenty feet, and then turned back as I twitched the fly. My fly line got all tangled and sunk too deeply.

"Easy, make small strips," Fly Bob instructed. "They think this fly is a bait fish, and if you get the right speed, they'll attack it."

I made a third cast upstream and concentrated on keep the fly drifting naturally with small strips of line. Another chum followed the fly downstream, and then it lost interest.

"I'll leave you to it." Fly Bob left me on my own for a while, probably getting the idea from the looks I was giving him from all his bossing around. For at least half an hour, I cast and cast with no luck.

Wasn't as easy as I thought.

Fly Bob pulled them in left and right. *Grrrrr,* it stinks when someone is catching and you're not. He waded in a little deeper with the help of his wading staff.

"Nature provides us some helpful tools," he shared. "I'll break off a dead branch and use it as a wading staff if I need one."

Even though it was deeper, I really wanted to catch a chum. So I found a sturdy stick and waded a little deeper than I wanted to. At least I wasn't up to my waist this time. Dad always reminded me to "figure things out" on the water. Every day, in every water system, the conditions changed for the fisherman. Dad prided himself on being among the 10 percent of anglers who caught 90 percent of the fish. The secret, he shared, was to be a versatile angler and be able to change with the conditions.

"The fish change with the conditions, so why shouldn't we?" Dad would use that analogy for real life, too. But the condition of him not being here seemed too much of a change for me to adapt to. How could I "figure things out" with this one?

He just wasn't coming back.

A gust of warmer wind blew on my cheeks and reminded me of what I was doing in the first place.

If I'm going to catch this slam, I need to focus and figure it out.

I pulled in my line and added another piece of split shot to weight the fly. Maybe I wasn't getting the fly down to them. I made another cast and just let it sit this time. A chum chewed it in.

I heaved my rod and soon felt the fury of the fish at the end of the line. The chum blew the water flat apart on the strike and headed downstream.

ZZZZZZZZZZZZZzzzzzzzzzzz! My reel unspooled fast, banged my knuckles, and scraped my skin. The chum took more and more of my fly line out until I realized it was headed into the end of my fly line backing. If I didn't get it under control, this thing would be headed back to the ocean.

Fly Bob called out instructions, and I held onto his rod for dear life.

OK, this isn't like fishing with wet flies at home.

"Keep your rod bent upstream, it'll turn his head," he shared. "Work him left, now right, now left. You're doing fine," he continued. "Keep the pressure on him. He might just tire out and slow down a little."

I listened to Fly Bob this time.

Eventually, that's just what the chum did. He settled way downstream about fifty yards from where we stood.

"Start reeling him back in now," Fly Bob directed as he leaned against the large stick he'd grabbed from shore.

"Walk him in as slow as he wants to come, just like you'd walk a dog!"

The power of the chum surged through the rod as I struggled to reel him back upstream. I pumped my rod back and forth to give myself some leverage as the fish neared.

Twenty feet, ten feet, five feet. I could now see the size of this chum. It had to be close to thirty inches long.

"Now swing him into the net. He's a good one."

The fish rolled over and into Fly Bob's awaiting net.

"Is he dead?"

"Nah, just really tired from fighting to stay alive!" Fly Bob unhooked the Everglow from its massive kype jaw.

"Now that's called walkin' the dog, buddy!" Fly Bob patted me on the back.

I handed Fly Bob my phone to take a pic and tried grabbing the salmon out of the net, but it wasn't so easy since he flopped around so much.

Finally, I reached under its belly and grasped its tail. I lifted it out of the net and kept the fish close to the water. This salmon had real teeth. Now I understood why they call them dog fish.

"Look at his chompers. OK, got the pic. Let 'em go. We'll catch some fresher ones."

I reluctantly placed the fish's head in the current. I had hoped Fly Bob was right about catching more. This was so different than catch and release at home. Here in Alaska, they practiced releasing fish, but only when they weren't 'good eating.' Seemed like we kept our limit only if the fish were silver and fresh in from the ocean. A lot different than 'catch and release' back home with native brookies.

The chum gained power quickly in the cold water, and twenty seconds later, he slapped his tail to propel forward.

As the day went on, I caught five more fish and kept three. The fish bite tapered off, but Fly Bob knew to switch things up a bit and tied on another fly.

"Check this one out. I call it the Popsicle."

Bob dangled a colorful fly made from various colors of marabou feathers.

"I tie in a lot of colors...it's supposed to mimic the salmon flesh. By now, most of the kings have spawned and died in this small river system. So the chums and big rainbow trout eat the salmon flesh pieces on their own way up to spawn."

It was one thing for the eagles, bear, and moose to eat the salmon flesh, but it seemed a little cannibalistic for the salmon to eat their own kind. Death seemed more and more normal to people up here in Alaska. I still found it disturbing.

We continued to fish as the sun hid beneath some cloud cover. A few more anglers entered the river before a storm rolled in quickly. I could hear the rain pounding on the trees. Fly Bob pulled out his raincoat and continued to cast. I did the same since it didn't bother the fish any. In fact, I liked fishing in the rain.

We even spotted a few bears along the trail. They seemed to leave us alone if we didn't have a salmon on our lines. One bear across the river, I named Mr. Fuzz, sat with his legs out and chowed down on a salmon carcass. I was close enough to see the rain droplets on his fur. He didn't mind either. I thought he looked a little cute, like a teddy bear. Fly Bob reminded me otherwise.

"Don't let these guys fool you. They'll come after you quick like you are a fast-food meal for them."

I spotted another blackish bear up high along the trail. Bob turned his head quickly as he closely observed all the bears.

"Know the best way to get away from a bear?" He asked. "Run faster than your friends!"

Dumb joke, but I had to admit, it was funny.

I hooked one fish that gave me a tremendous ten-minute fight. As I was bringing him to the net, Fly Bob abruptly cut my line and started backing me up.

"What did you do that for?" I griped.

"Look below you and get moving."

The black bear that was once up above us was now down along the trail, coming toward us. I reached for my phone in my backpack, but Fly Bob grabbed my hood quickly and dragged me up to the next hole. He dropped the two stringers of our fish back in deeper water and flipped the end of the rope on a bush, probably so the bear wouldn't see them. Luckily, there was a family of three people up ahead, making us look like a formidable bunch to the bear.

Bob raised his hands and said, "GO BEAR. GO BEAR!" I followed his lead and did the same. The family quickly understood the bear situation and joined in to yell as well.

The black bear stopped, sniffed, and tried to circle above us.

I knew that he wasn't hunting us and just wanted a meal, but my heart rate jumped when the bear was so close. We waited for a while until the bear found its way upstream and was a safe distance away.

"Promised your mom we'd be safe, so you gotta keep your head on a swivel with these guys!"

My gut agreed.

"I can always tell the tourists from the locals," said Fly Bob. "When a bear shows up, the locals back away, and the tourists pull their cameras out and move closer."

I thought that last comment was for me since Fly Bob walked away a little perturbed. He resumed fishing mode and motioned me downstream to fish below him. We both hooked into a few more chums into the evening, even though I couldn't tell with the sun still hiding behind the clouds. I hooked one monster chum, and he helped me get it to the net.

"Yeah, we call these 'Chromers' since they're fresh in from the ocean," Bob explained. "But they still have some energy, don't they? They have this beautiful silver chrome on their scales. Eventually, this will change when they hit the freshwater. Too bad we already have our limit on the stringers. Let 'em go."

I had forgotten that we each had three on the stringer, our daily limit. I wanted to keep this one, but it's illegal to remove one from the stringer and put another one on it. I had to respect that Fly Bob followed the Alaskan fishing rules.

Fly Bob helped me remove the Popsicle fly without hooking myself. I knelt down and released the salmon back into the water. Fly Bob took a good photo of me releasing the fish. It was one of my favorites since it wasn't the usual 'grip-and-grin.'

The chum reenergized, whipping its tail back and forth as a signal it was ready to go. I moved my hands away from the fish and watched as it rejoined the other chums headed upstream.

"Where are they going?" I asked Fly Bob.

"They're headed upstream. They'll reproduce and eventually die. That's the life of a salmon, born in freshwater, head out to the ocean for a few years, and then come back to their birth stream to mate. Then they die."

What a waste. These fish make it all the way back into their home waters just to lay eggs and die.

"That seems like an unhappy ending," I expressed.

"Yeah, I guess it's all in how you look at it. After they spawn and die, they become food for the rest of the stream, for bears, eagles, other fish, and especially the salmon fry and fingerlings that must grow into adults. Everything would be a shadow of what it is if it weren't for these salmon."

He grabbed the stringers, the six chums, and we walked further downstream to a table sitting in the middle of the stream.

"Let's start filleting these chums up."

"Why is this table here in the middle of the river?" I asked.

"This keeps the bears away when we drop the guts into deeper water. Even the guts of these fish we caught will add to the animals' meals tonight. We make the best of the whole salmon."

Fly Bob sliced through the chum's scales, grabbed some guts, and threw the fish entrails and bones into deeper water. He cut four fillets out of each fish, washed his hands in the water, and wiped the blade off on his waders. Gross, but he really knew how to fillet a salmon quickly.

"So really," he continued, "if they didn't die, they wouldn't leave room for the next generation. See how the fish already started feeding on the leftovers." He pointed to a few rainbows moving up into the channel to eat the flesh.

"I see it as a pretty purposeful life." Fly Bob squinted and looked up into the rainy mist as he started to cut another chum. "Helping others live their lives...kind of a good way to go if you ask me."

My heart skipped a beat.

After that, I couldn't pay much attention to anything but the rotting salmon carcasses. Across the river, I spotted a bald eagle picking out red pieces of salmon flesh from a bony carcass. Swimming around my feet, smaller trout fed on micro particles of salmon. Even the tall trees surrounding the landscape seemed to sip from the river.

So many other creatures' life cycles depended on the salmon. Dad was like that. People depended on him. We depended on him.

People loved him.

I love him.

I imagined Dad as a salmon fighting the currents.

Would he make the journey upstream knowing that it would eventually end in his own death?

Redds Cooper would do that for others, and especially for Mom and me to live on, to survive.

Now it was time to give something back to him.

I. ~~CHUM~~

II. ~~RED~~

III. KING

IV. SILVER

V. PINK

Two down and three fish to go.

CHAPTER 9

July 11th — 6:26 a.m.

Dear Dad,

Headed out to try for the King today. Some of the guides said they saw some pods in the Kenai yesterday. Will ask Fly Bob if he can take me again and try to get one toward the slam.

Didn't need the alarm to get up this morning, as I wouldn't be late for Fly Bob this time. I was on a mission.

He had clients again but said I could tag along and fish the Russian River with them. The Pinks and Silvers wouldn't be running until later in the month, so the King was my target. Mom decided to stay back and work on the book. Now that we had our bear lesson, I think it helped her let me go without her.

I walked over to the convenience store to pick up the necessities for the day trip: Gatorade, beef jerky, a banana, a Lenny 'Laskan Root Beer, and of course, my favorite candy bar, an almond Hershey chocolate bar. Always one of Dad's favorites, he packed them all the time in our cooler for the midday snack. As long as it stayed cool, it didn't melt in our packs. He'd always got Mom a Dark Chocolate Hershey bar to take back home.

Once in a while, we'd forget one was in there and come home with a squishy Hershey bar.

Fly Bob stood in front of Gwin's with his two clients, all wadered up. Luckily, I was ready to go, and we set off for the Russian River Trail again. We passed by the same trees, and Fly Bob told his same stories. We stopped at the watering hole and filled up our canteens. We even stopped to look at bear tracks and scat. That's when Bob gave his clients 'the talk' about watching out for bears. I really wasn't as scared as I was last time. Didn't seem to be many around to be scared of anyway.

We headed downhill toward the river, and when we got to the water's edge, Fly Bob pointed me to the next pool downstream. He moved his clients up into a nice hole. I think he felt better that I was in sight.

An eagle perched across the stream on a boulder chewing on a salmon carcass. Seeing eagles up here as scavengers really didn't make me feel good about them being a symbol for American freedom. The bird ripped another a piece of salmon meat off the bone and chewed it. I had to take a picture of that.

I rigged my rod and tied on a cream Flesh Fly. Fly Bob said we should "match the hatch" today so I picked a color of fly that matches the salmon flesh coming down the stream from rotting carcasses. After a few casts, I had a chase or two, but I couldn't hook into anything.

Being sure not to wade too much further in, I took a few steps down stream and made another cast.

A few hours went by without a bite, but I wasn't giving up. It took me another hour, but I started to get the feel for the river. I saw more flashes after my fly, signaling fish swimming by.

Fish on!

I hooked, played, and reeled in a pretty nice rainbow, about 16 inches. Would've been a beast compared to Pennsylvania trout. I tried to get a picture of the spotted pink and green sides, but it flipped out of my hands and splashed its way back into the currents.

A dark brown bear on the other side of the river made an appearance and snorted. I named him Mr. Dark Hershey. He sniffed in the air, waiting for the smells to arrive at his snout. His fur coat looked scraggly and matted.

Even though the bear was close, I kept fishing since I saw a few flashes.

Fish on, again! I could tell was a bigger fish by the bow in my rod. *Maybe it's a King this time?*

It spooled off some line, so I tried leading it to shore. It made a leap and surge, and then broke my line off with a tremendous splash and took the fly with it. My reel drag was set too tight, so I made an adjustment for the next time.

Another light brownish shape burst out of the brush on my side of the river. It was a different bear, but closer. Dad's camo hat flipped off my head as I turned around to spot it. I grabbed for the hat, but it fell into the current. The brown bear with a lighter shade of Hershey walked closer to me, and I spotted Mr. Dark Hershey swimming upstream towards me.

I tried to reach for Dad's hat as it floated downstream. I heard Fly Bob yell, but I couldn't lose that hat, so I kept wading deeper to grab it. I finally flipped my fly line into the current and hooked the hat on the end of my fly.

Great snag! Some water got into my waders, but I was able to back up and got into more shallow water.

BOOM! BOOM!

I looked up to see Fly Bob standing with his gun drawn in the air, the pistol barrel still smoking. He had fired over Mr. Dark Hershey's head and screamed at both bears. The lighter Hershey bear was clearly startled and bolted for the woods, but Mr. Dark Hershey merely strolled on the trail back downstream as we stood our ground.

We waited in silence until the bear disappeared around the bend. I reeled in Dad's hat and unhooked it from the fly.

"Jack, you can't fool around with these bears," Fly Bob scolded. "This is life and death."

"But I had to get..."

Fly Bob cut me off, "No buts about it, it's just a hat. Let it go."

"No, it's not! You wouldn't understand."

"Oh yeah? I understand your father wouldn't want you chasing a silly hat in place of your life."

"Well, you're not my father!"

Fly Bob made a gruff sound and headed back up with his clients, but not before pointing to a boulder on shore and motioning me to sit there. "I want you safe where I can see you, understand?" He said firmly, leaving no room for argument.

I sat on the shore while he instructed the two anglers.

A soaking wet kid in time-out. I pulled out my journal and vented to Dad.

July 11th — 2:17 p.m.

Dear Dad,

I'm as wet as a dog. Had a close call with some bears — Mr. Hershey and Mr. Dark Hershey bears. Didn't realize they were so close. Really have to be alert for them. Fly Bob wasn't too happy with me, but who cares? At least I saved your camo hat.

Really thought I had a King on. That woulda made it three fish for the slam. Man, I really wanted to get one in. Trying my best to get it, but it's hard.

Will keep you posted.

After walking back to the cabins with Fly Bob and his clients, we saw Mom had started a campfire in the pit. The fire blazed against a blue horizon. The chilly evening air vanished and surprisingly the atmosphere filled with a nice warm breeze.

"Hey guys, beautiful night for a campfire, right?" Mom grinned. "I thought I'd grill up some of the salmon you guys caught the other day. Made some salmon burgers with lettuce, onion, and tomato."

"Wow, thanks Jill. That's was thoughtful of you. Yum." Fly Bob dug into the meal.

I didn't want to tell her that Fly Bob and I had a little incident, so I sat quietly on a log near the fire to dry off. Fly Bob seemed to take the cue and did the same thing while eating his burger.

Mom noticed the tension and asked, "How was the fishing today?"

Fly Bob shared first. "Great day on the water. Avoided a few bears, too."

Good one, old man.

"Well, I was able to meet with the game warden today. He said we could join a class about Alaskan wildlife this week down at the Sanctuary. Thought it would be great for the book, right Jack?"

I nodded and chewed my burger.

"I'll take that as a 'Yes Mom, the class sounds fun,'" she teased.

We finished the meal without having to recap the day for Mom.

She made small talk with Fly Bob about Cooper Landing, but her look told me she knew something was up.

Mom gave a big yawn. "I'm headed to the cabin for some sleep. Jack, if you want to stay up later, feel free. Don't forget, we have the Kenai River float trip tomorrow morning."

Then she left before I could even get up.

That left Fly Bob and me alone.

The campfire seemed to spark the conversation since we could both stare into the fire instead of each other.

We sat on logs and listened to the fire hiss and the wolves howl off in the distance.

Fly Bob spoke first. "I remember your dad and me would have campfires almost every night. We'd laugh about how many fish we caught and who fell in and all kinds of things."

I missed campfires with my dad, too. He really did love them.

"He always had a way of keeping the fire burning hot until the morning." I shared.

Bob stoked the fire. "Yep, wish I could just tell him I missed him."

Thunder rolled off in the distance.

"Did you always live here with Dad?" I asked.

"Your father spent his first five years up here in Alaska living with your grandmother and me. We went fishing and hiking, just like the two of you did back home. Then we ended up moving down to the lower forty-eight...'er, rather Pennsylvania, for your grandma's career."

I kept staring at the fire, and Fly Bob kept spilling his guts.

Keep going.

"We were a happy family, but the more I was away from Alaska, the more I missed guiding. You know when something grabs you, it doesn't let go. I needed to be here on the water."

"So you left your family?" It was a natural reaction for me to ask that question, but I regretted it right away because Fly Bob flinched like I'd punched him in the stomach.

He strained to share the next part, and his voice was barely audible. "I separated from your grandmother and ended up moving back here to Cooper Landing. Redds stayed in Pittsburgh with his mother. He visited me every summer until he headed off to college to become a writer. That's when we lost touch with each other."

I saw the fire reflect off a tear as it rolled silently down his cheek. Fly Bob wiped his eyes on the cuff of his jacket and continued.

"Your dad flew back to Alaska one last time to introduce your mom to me before you were born. Right away, I knew they'd get married, which they did. I missed the wedding. I could never get myself on those flying death traps."

Excuses.

I wondered if he could see my eyes roll in the dark.

"Then a few months after that your grandmother died. I didn't come down for her funeral. Redds told me never to speak to him again. He was sad and hurt since I didn't come to the wedding or his mom's funeral. I knew we were both stubborn, so I thought it best if I didn't come back to Pennsylvania, ever. I decided to just let things be. It was a mistake. I always wanted to talk to your father and say I was sorry."

Adults can be so thick when things could be easier.

"Since he was working on the book, we both felt it would make a good story if we could make things right again between us. I made a lot of mistakes, Jack, but having a family wasn't one of them. I just wish I coulda done right by your dad. I did write him though." His voice trailed off.

I just nodded because I didn't really know what to say.

We both stared at the campfire a little longer.

"I see a lot of your father in you – sometimes it's hard to be around you. Reminds me too much of him."

I nodded. "Yeah, same with you," I shared.

"Jack, I'm sorry I yelled at you today. I just didn't want anything to happen to you."

I could tell it was hard for him to apologize. I guess that's a genetic Cooper trait.

"I'm sorry, too. I just couldn't let Dad's hat go."

The fire crackled some more in the silence.

"I need your help catching the slam." I asked in a weird sort of way. "I'm serious about doing it this summer for Dad."

Fly Bob looked up from the fire and stood to stretch.

"Of course, I'm here to help. Reminds me of happier times."

With that, he patted me on the back and walked back to his trailer.

"Well, I'm headed in for the night. G'night."

I took the cue that our campfire conversation had ended. I sat at the embers a little bit longer and stared up into the sky.

I thought of Benny then and how, in his own way, he'd tried to make things right in his life again.

Maybe helping me catch the Salmon Slam would be Fly Bob's way of making it right, too.

CHAPTER 10

ALASKAN ☆
FACTS:

☆ ☆
☆ ☆
☆ ☆
☆ ☆

When salmon are spawning,
Rainbow Trout feed on their eggs.
When salmon decay & die,
trout change their diet to eating the
rotting salmon flesh.

I peered down from the loft. Mom was still sound asleep below. I woke without the alarm clock this morning, too excited. Fishing is a natural alarm clock. I remember sleeping with my fishing clothes on the night before a trip so I wouldn't miss a minute with Dad.

Mom and I were scheduled to take a drift trip together down the mighty Kenai River. With the outside chance of getting into a King for the slam, I was geared and ready to go.

I grabbed my tackle and sling pack, softly woke Mom, and headed outside to check on the temps. Outside of his trailer, Fly Bob stood with a hot cup of something steaming in the brisk Alaskan air.

"Why are you up so early?" I asked.

"Gotta love these mountains," Fly Bob answered, keeping his gaze at the sky. "Look at how the clouds float through them. Like God's big white kites."

We stood in silence watching the cloud wisps dance over the mountains.

"Think it'll be a good fishing day?"

Fly Bob took a sip from his 'The River Is My Office' mug. "Son, every day in Alaska is a good day to fish!"

"We're taking a drift boat down the Kenai today." I said more excitedly than I wanted.

"Yes, different kind of fishing, but you'll love fishing for weighty rainbows. You might even tag into that King."

That prospect sounded good. I wanted to get back on track with the slam.

"I think you're going out with Gill. He's a great boat handler and one 'fishy' guy. You'll have a stellar day on the K."

Mom and I met Gill at the head of the Kenai River Dam. Gill looked like any of the other guides with beard scruff, a ball cap that had a trout on it, and his Simms waders. Mom and I were all bundled up for the morning sixty-degree temperatures, but he wore just a t-shirt which read: 'HOOKED on SALMON!'

I couldn't help but dip my hands into the frigid and silted water. It was an emerald color, almost the color of the ocean in the Caribbean. The cold water dried out my skin like sand polishing a stone.

Gill rigged up our rods with plastic beads instead of flies.

"Why a bead?" Mom asked.

"Well, the bead simulates a salmon egg. These females are so full of eggs when they're spawning that all the fish species key in on the eggs." Gill said.

"It's pegged a little above the hook," Gill continued, "so the fish don't engulf it. They usually swallow these eggs deep in their gullets, so this is a better technique to catch them in their mouth. It's kind of a fishing regulation rule up here in Alaska. These salmon and rainbows are sometimes so picky when it comes to the colors. Us guides keep a lot of these bead colors to try out."

Gill pulled out a bunch of bead boxes from the boat. I counted more than fifty colors of pinks, peaches, creams, reds, and whites. Amazing that fish would go after round pieces of plastic. They did look remarkably like the salmon eggs I saw at the hatchery, though.

He pegged the bead a little way up the line and tied the hook below it. Definitely a different way of fishing, but if it works, that's good for us.

Gill then packed up the remaining duffle bags in the drift boat, handed us life jackets, and said, "OK, put these on, and we're off." He pushed the oars deep in the current, and we moved off shore and into the currents.

The Kenai River was two football fields wide, if not three. The evergreens and spruce trees lined the banks as we observed what seemed to be white heads atop every other tree.

"Wow, those are all bald eagles." Mom recognized.

"Yep, we have a lot of them up here fighting the bears over salmon carcasses. They swoop down quickly to get their meals. Hey, that reminds me, I have something for you, Jack," Gill said, pulling out a long black leather strip from his boat box.

"The guides around here say if you have an eagle eye, you'll have a great fishing season. Figured it would help you on your Salmon Slam."

"Wow, cool." I thanked him. Looking down, I rubbed my finger tips over the image of a bald eagle, wings spread wide open that was etched into the leather. It looked long enough to be a book mark, so I tucked it in my Alaskan journal.

As we bounced our bead rigs downstream in the current, Mom's indicator shot upstream right away. Her rod bent over as she held onto it tightly. The rainbow on the end of the line did a few leaps. This wasn't your ordinary rainbow trout, but a hefty monster! Bob was right.

"Keep that 'C' in your rod upstream. Make that bow work against the current." Gill advised.

Mom worked the fish back and forth with a grin as wide as the river.

Gill grabbed the net and reached underneath to pull the beast from the water.

"Woohoo," Mom yelled.

Just then, my line also ripped upstream, and I had a rainbow on.

"Doubles," I called.

Gill anchored the drift boat while I worked the bow back and forth. Since I'd had all that practice on the salmon, this rainbow seemed to hook itself. I knew I had him under control from his headshaking.

The bow surfaced, and I led him to Gill's net with Mom's fish still in it.

Whoosh! Gill scooped up my fish.

"That's a lot of trout weight," he laughed. "Let's get to shore and get a good pic. Hold this, Jack."

I held the netted fish in the water while Gill lifted anchor and headed to the nearest bank. Mom smiled at me and winked. She was into this whole experience. It felt like a win for both of us.

Gill was just as excited as we were to get that double picture shot. I guess that's the difference between a good fishing guide and a great one. He showed us how to release each fish so they could live to eat more eggs. Mine made a huge splash.

Suddenly, a crash from the bushes caught our attention. We turned to see an emerging black figure. The black bear waddled its way over to us looking for a handout. I still couldn't help naming them, so I called this one, Mr. Darth Vader.

"Get into the boat," Gill instructed, before moving in to put himself between us and Vader Bear.

The dark trickster sniffed and snorted. Then it turned its head, as if trying to sniff us out.

"GO BEAR!" Gill hollered, and we joined in, waiving with our hands over our heads to look taller and meaner. I felt like we were the Ewoks in Return of the Jedi waving hands and yelling at the Stormtroopers.

The beast took a step toward us and then decided to walk down the coastline after hearing another splash downstream.

"That was close," Gill chuckled. "These guys are always looking for an easy meal, and I try not to give it to them."

"Just glad it wasn't us," Mom added.

"We have a slogan that a 'fed bear' is a 'dead bear,' which means that if you feed one, the local ranger will have to put it down since it will become too aggressive and unafraid of people. So, guides don't ever feed the bears with salmon or any other food."

Gill hopped back in the boat, pushed off with the oars, and we sailed down the Kenai once again. The spruce trees lining the river sped by as we held our rods and enjoyed the brisk air. I definitely got more scenery pictures to add to the book on this drift trip.

I would estimate we each caught about five more rainbows. Though I thought it was a King, one rainbow I caught was so beefy and gorged that when Gill held it up, eggs spilled out of its mouth.

When we finished the trip in the early evening, Mom gave Gill a generous guide's tip for his efforts and invited him to the restaurant to have a late dinner with us.

We met Fly Bob there and had fried salmon patties.

By now, I think I'd had salmon cooked in all the ways Gwin's could invent.

CHAPTER 11

July 15th — 7:12 a.m.

Hey Dad.

Sorry it's been a few days since I've written. We've been busy hiking and trying out new flies.

Fly Bob is taking me to catch some kind of trout with weird fins. I'll let you know how it goes…hopefully, we'll get Mom to fish today, too.

Still trying to catch the K.

Salmo barged into the cabin first and awakened Mom with nose nudges. Then I overheard Fly Bob's booming voice below in the kitchen.

"Well, no clients to fish with today, so I have the whole day free," Bob shared with Mom. "I was wondering if y'all would like to go to a special little stream of mine and do some easy fishin'. You might get some good details for your book."

Luckily, I had prepped Fly Bob to entice Mom to come today since she hadn't been out fishing much, other than the float trip. I sat up in bed and waited for Mom's response. Ever since Dad died, Mom was hesitant to go near the water, let alone fish. It probably was too painful for her.

Could Fly Bob convince her to join us?

"Well, if I'm finishing this Alaskan Guidebook, I should log more time on the water and do some real Alaskan fly fishing," She reflected.

I shot out of bed, grabbed my rod, and climbed down the ladder.

"I'm ready when you are!"

Even though we weren't going for salmon, I thought it was good for us all to get out, especially for Mom. Besides, I might just luck out and hook into a King for the slam.

Off we went in Fly Bob's rusty pickup truck. The three of us sat in the front of the cab while Salmo paced excitedly in the truck bed. Bob drove many miles before turning off the pavement onto a deserted gravel road with no sign.

"These back-country roads are almost impassable in the wintertime with all the snow that falls, and they don't get paved since the ice and snow would just break them up. The only vehicles that can pass through here in winter are the snow machines."

I imagined gigantic snow machines with wheels as big as my house plowing through the snow.

"I think you folks in the lower forty-eight call them 'snow mobiles,' right?"

Mom looked at me, and we laughed. She thought the same thing. Man, it was good to see her smile.

"You think that's funny? Many Alaskans also call 'em 'snow-goes,' too," Fly Bob added.

We giggled again.

Bob pointed out the glacial stream that paralleled the road, running several feet below. It looked muddy and gray to me, like in my dream.

The old truck passed by hundreds of acres of evergreens on both sides of the road and mountains that stretched off into the distance. A few times, I had to yawn to pop my eardrums since our altitude changed so many times along the way.

Fly Bob finally stopped at a bridge overlooking a clear creek that ran beneath and led into the larger glacial river.

"We're here," Bob announced with a magical look of excitement in his eyes that all anglers get when they get to a stream.

He walked to the back of the truck and unloaded some gear, handing one rod to Mom and one to me. They were rigged to go already – one with a nymph and one with a streamer. Then he hoisted a rifle over his shoulder with his sidearm still attached to his belt.

"OK, a few words of caution before we head out," Bob asserted. I remembered this talk from before, but this time, Fly Bob seemed even more serious and stern. The rifle surely had something to do with his seriousness, too.

"Out here, the wildlife isn't as used to having humans stomping around on their turf, so they sometimes can be a little unpredictable and aggressive. Usually, if we give them notice and make enough noise, they'll find their way around us.

"I want you both to keep your eyes n' ears open for anything around us, especially on the trail, since it's the only way to get in or out. If you hear me whistle, that'll be the sign to be aware of your surroundings. Salmo usually will give us advance notice if any bear or moose are around, and I'll be on the ready," he affirmed, patting his rifle, "so we shouldn't have any problems."

I felt a mix of excitement, fear, and wonder, like I did while waiting in line for the big roller coaster at the amusement park back home.

Fly Bob continued, "The good news is these graylings haven't seen any fishing since last season, so they'll be hungry and ready to strike!"

I liked the sound of that, especially for Mom.

"What are grayling?" She asked.

"Well, they're really like trout," Bob explained, "but they have an extended dorsal fin and scales like a carp. They can live in the coldest of water too, and they love to eat artificial flies. Let's go get 'em."

We walked a little way through the dense brush. These weren't human trails, but more likely those of the animals that traveled along the creek. Thickets, plants, and bushes seemed to choke the path.

When I spotted a pile of scat at my feet, Fly Bob confirmed it was only moose droppings. It looked like a cow patty, unlike the small hard nuggets I'd seen in pictures. Apparently, the type of food source significantly changed the appearance of moose scat in winter compared to summer.

As we reached a small riffle of the creek that led into a larger pool, Fly Bob explained how to catch this fish called a grayling.

"Now, you have a Black Bear Nymph on, so you just want to float that baby downstream like it's a fly caught in the current. I tied that with some real black bear fur. You'll feel the fish take it, and then you'll have to set the hook."

He imitated tugging his rod upward.

"Take a few steps in the water and make a cast upstream."

I waved Mom into the prime casting spot in the pool, and Fly Bob acknowledged my generosity with a nod of his head.

She stood at the gravel edge for a while. Then for the first time here in Alaska, she openly sobbed in front of us. I walked over to Mom and leaned into her.

I didn't say much. What could I possibly say to make it all better? No words ever made me feel any better.

We ended up sitting down on the gravel and hugging each other.

After a few minutes, Mom rose to her feet, wiped her eyes, and took a step into the stream. Fly Bob and I kept quiet.

She made a decent enough cast upstream so that her fly had time to float downstream. As if on cue, her rod broke into a twitching frenzy from a grayling on the end of her line that quickly.

Fly Bob noticed she was pointing her rod at the fish the way every novice fly fisherman did, but before he could give her any advice, I chimed in, "Lift your rod tip, Mom!"

She lifted her rod up with excitement and began hooting and hollering.

"Well, looks like you scared the bears away." Fly Bob teased.

She led the grayling into Fly Bob's waiting wet hands.

"Great job, Mom," I said. "Now that's a nice-looking fish."

"That's for your father," Mom proudly announced.

Fly Bob held the fish in his hands. In all the time I've fished, I'd never seen one before. The grayling had bluish iridescent sides with a tint of rainbow coloring. What made it unique was its large dorsal fin, which Bob proudly lifted and displayed for Mom. I took a picture.

"Let's catch some more!" I urged.

Salmo barked with excitement, too.

"Hey Mom, Dad would be proud of you."

With teary eyes, she gave me a loving smile and nodded.

All that day, we caught grayling after grayling. I think Mom caught even more than me or Fly Bob. Mom became a quick pro at handling the fish and releasing them just as easily.

I even tied on an Adam's dry fly that I'd brought from PA. Fly Bob was surprised that the grayling went crazy over it as I floated it on the water's surface. This kind of fishing reminded me of the bluegills and sunfish I fished for back home with Dad in the neighbor's pond. The grayling loved biting at the surface and readily took in the dry fly.

"Hey, what fly you using over there?" Bob asked.

"Is Fly Bob asking me what fly to use?" I joked.

I pulled one out and shared it with him. He'd certainly shared enough flies with me this summer.

"Leave it to a Pennsylvania kid to know how to dry fly fish." Bob chuckled.

"Here, got another fly to share with you." Fly Bob rooted through his pack and came up with a fly that looked like a pattern from home.

"This is a version of the Elk Hair Caddis, only I tie it up using the Caribou hide. Even though it's lighter colored, it works really well in the cloudy conditions like today." He handed me a few Caribou Caddis flies, and I put them into my fly box for later.

Though I didn't concentrate on catching the Salmon Slam that day, it was one of the most memorable days of the summer, especially spending time with Mom. She even said she might add a section in the book about fishing for grayling in the Kenai Peninsula area.

I never knew fishing with her could be so much fun, and I wished we'd invited her more when we were a family of three.

When we get back home, I promised myself to invite her to our secret spot more often.

CHAPTER 12

ALASKAN ☆
FACTS:

☆ ☆ ☆
☆ ☆
☆
☆ ☆

The Alaskan Wood Frog (*Rana sylvatica*)
freezes during the winter.
While frozen, it stops breathing, its heart
stops beating, its blood stops flowing, &
it can't move.

July 17th — 10:06 a.m.

Dear Dad,

Mom and I are headed down the Sanctuary today for a class on Alaskan wildlife. We get to take the Russian River Ferry again, so I'm looking forward to it.

Definitely will be watching out for the bears!

Mom and I took the morning to sleep in. I still got the pancakes at the Lodge though.

We took 'Ole Blue' down to the Russian River Ferry area again, rode the ferry over, and hiked up to the Sanctuary for the class. Fly Bob had a client day to fish, so my plan was to go with Mom to the class and maybe get some afternoon fishing in by the Sanctuary.

Misty rain draped over the Kenai River area like a wet blanket locking in all the moisture. The air had a drizzly sting to it that found its way through the seams in my old rain jacket. Dad was an advocate of having quality fishing gear, including rain jackets. Mom seemed to be fine walking in the new jacket she'd purchased before we left for the trip.

Except for a handful of anglers, the riverbanks were empty. I asked the ferry captain, this time an older lady in a flannel shirt named Corhyn, why there were no fishermen.

"The reds have made their second run upriver already, so there's not many fish in the river but rainbows." Corhyn said. "The humpies should be the next big event down at the mouth, and I hope they hurry because I'm bored just sittin' here. Hopefully, they'll be running in the next few weeks, and everybody will be back."

I noticed she'd left out the King run since we were so far out from that. Still, I had prepared my fly box with all the king-worthy flies; I had my rod with me, intending to fish after.

We hiked to the tip of Sanctuary Island, and a few more people had braved the cooler temperatures and rain by then to hear Ranger Rick's presentation. OK, that wasn't his real name, but the ranger title reminded me of all the Ranger Rick magazines I'd read as a kid.

The class was made up of a lady in a pink cowboy hat, an older man and woman, a Dad, Mom, and three little kids, and Mom and me. I noticed that Corhyn, the ferry captain, even joined us.

The ranger recognized me right away from the moose incident and said, "Hey 'Moose Man,' how are you recovering?"

It was kind of embarrassing, but since he'd helped me in the beginning of the summer, I smirked and laughed it off. Now that I'd been around for nearly three weeks, my head was 'on a swivel' as I looked out for the wildlife.

The ranger led us to an outdoor seating area with logs as seats, kind of an outdoor classroom. The first Alaskan animal he shared with the class was the Wood Frog. He even had these laminated cards which included the scientific names. It was pretty impressive.

'Wood Frog' (AKA *Rana sylvatica*). My dad and I always liked reading the genus and species names of the animals at the Carnegie Museum. The "two-names" he used to say.

"This guy is really special to Alaska," the ranger shared. "In the winter, the Wood Frog digs a shallow hole and covers itself with leaves and debris. It slows down its breathing, its heart, and its metabolism. This is to deal with the extreme cold temperatures we get up here. Basically, it becomes a frog

Popsicle."

He paused for some laughter, and the group obliged.

"When spring rolls around, his body thaws, and the creature warms from the inside out to return to a normal life."

Ranger Rick carefully passed the live Wood Frog around to us. When I held it, I stared into its eyes before taking a quick picture. Even though he wasn't frozen, he stayed still in my hand.

I thought it was pretty interesting I'd been feeling the same way recently.

Too bad humans couldn't freeze themselves and thaw out when they wanted to.

The ranger's next artifact was an eagle's wing (*Haliaeetus leucocephalus*). It had to be at least 3 feet across.

I recognized the eagle feathers right away and thought of the eagle we'd seen with Gill.

"Alaska has about 30,000 bald eagles," said Ranger Rick. "That's the largest population of bald eagles in the US. They have a wingspan of up to seven and a half feet. Their main diet is fish," he continued. "Eagles can actually float pretty well with a thick down of feathers. Sometimes, an eagle will grab a fish that's too heavy and tow the meat to shore rather than fly with it. They're seen not only as scavengers and predators, but also as a symbol to the Alaskan native's way before they became the American national emblem in 1782."

Next, the ranger said, "So a question I get a lot up here is: 'What's the difference between a Black Bear and a Grizzly?'" He held up some plastic bear track molds. "One way to tell the difference is by the front toes. The toes of this track form an arc. That's when you can tell it's a Black Bear. The Grizzly Bear's paw has more of a straight toe line. Another difference is in their claws. Black Bears have short dark claws and grizzlies have long, light claws."

The ranger passed around the claws on a rope, to the oohs and ahhs of the audience.

"The Grizzly Bear has more of a muscle between its shoulders giving the appearance of a hump. Black bears don't have a hump. This enables

Grizzlies to be powerful diggers to excavate dens, root out vegetation, and swipe at salmon."

I remembered the grizzly (*Ursus arctos*) swiping after my salmon. After his main presentation, the ranger allowed us to look through all the bins of animals, pelts, and skulls. Mom pulled a bear skull out of the ranger's bin and held it in her hands.

"Can you tell which type of bear that is?" The ranger asked.

"I'm guessing it's the Black bear since it has a thinner face," she responded.

"You got it! The Grizzly Bear skull has a much broader head."

Ranger Rick soon gathered us all together to wrap up the class.

Dad was right – nature is a great classroom. I even forgot it was a class.

"Thanks for being a great audience in the rain," Ranger Rick concluded. "I'd like to leave you with an Alaskan legend from the Haida Nation of Southeast Alaska called 'Salmon Boy.' I'm not the best at retelling stories, so I asked Corhyn to share her tribe's legend. I feel it really speaks to respecting salmon and showing stewardship for all living creatures and our wonderful Alaska waters."

On makeshift seats fashioned from large tree trunks, we sat in a circle to listen to Corhyn tell the tale of the 'Salmon Boy.'

"This story is about a young boy who showed no respect for the Salmon People or their undersea home," she began.

"When his elders taught their people to take care of the salmon they caught, the boy did not. He threw them onto the rocks and trampled over them.

"When the elders taught their village families to place the salmon bones back into the water after they ate them as a sign of honor and gratitude, the boy did not. He carelessly threw the bones on the ground and into the bushes.

I thought back to Fly Bob being sure to return every salmon bone to the water.

"When the elders taught the children to respect the river's power and stay close to the shore when the river was high, the boy did not. He swam out to the middle of the river to taunt the other children.

"One rainy day, the boy swam out too far into the river, and the currents took him down into the depths."

Corhyn glanced over at me, and I flashbacked to my dream of drowning.

"There, he met the Salmon People. They had left their salmon bodies behind for the villagers, the animals, and everything living thing around, and returned to their home deep in the river depths. Now, the boy belonged to the Salmon People, and they took him with them.

"When he arrived in the ocean, the Salmon People looked like humans. He saw that their village was much like his own with elders, families, and children. Over the winter, the Salmon People taught the boy many lessons. He learned how important it was to return the salmon to the waters to protect the Salmon children and keep them alive. Eventually, they named him 'Salmon Boy.' He learned to live with respect, honor, and gratitude.

"When it was time for the Salmon People to journey back upriver to spawn in the spring, they invited to the Salmon Boy to join them. As he swam past his own village, his mother scooped him up in her salmon net. He shed his salmon skin and revealed himself. His village had many sick people, and Salmon Boy healed them and shared the wisdom of the Salmon People with them. When it was his time to die, he made the village elders promise to return him to the river, where his soul floated out to sea to remain forever with the Salmon People. To this day, my people respect the lessons of the Salmon People, to care for the salmon, each other, and everything around us."

We all clapped for Corhyn and the lessons from the Salmon boy. Then everyone dispersed and headed back to the ferry.

When the ranger noticed I had my fishing gear, he told me that he saw the Pinks down at the river mouth earlier. Seemed like everyone knew I was trying for the slam.

Since no one was really fishing, I asked Mom if I could have an hour or two to cast, and she agreed. I tied on a Coho Fly that Fly Bob had whipped up yesterday and let it glide in the downstream current. Mom sat and wrote notes for the book while I flung my rod back and forth without any luck.

I reflected on the Corhyn's story and how everything in Alaska was so entwined with salmon. It seemed like all the Alaskan creatures had to tough it out in this place, even the small Wood Frog.

We had a lot in common.

Freeze. Warm. Defrost.

In truth, Alaska had thawed me out a little and helped me enjoy fishing again. I was like the Salmon Boy when I came, but after spending some time and learning, I could really see how everything in this place was linked. Life and death were important to the big picture, especially when the salmon helped everything else survive.

Speaking of which, the humpies were in.

CHAPTER 13

Another early wake-up.

I rubbed my eyes as Fly Bob drove me to the mouth of the river.

"It's worth getting up for, kid."

So this is what it takes to catch the slam.

"You're one lucky fella," Bob added. "Not only is this an even year where the pinks are comin,' but the rains that lasted all night raised the river. That should bring those pinks in from the ocean. I think we might just get your third fish of the slam today."

We drove the Sterling Highway a long way to the Homer mouth where the ocean met the river. So many fishermen waded in the water like houses lined up along the river.

Then, like dancing sailboats, I saw their fins sliced through the water. Hundreds upon hundreds of humpbacked pinks made their way into the fresh water to spawn. Their small developing humps rose to the surface. The fishermen all knew they'd be here.

Eerily, the scene reminded me of my dream and stepping across fish like they were stones to reach Dad. My jaw dropped. I couldn't even count the number of salmon that clogged the river's mouth. They moved through the water, at times carrying the entire surface with them.

"Pretty amazing, huh?" said Fly Bob, interrupting my thoughts. "Bet you haven't seen anything like this in Pennsylvania."

I agreed and followed Bob down the trail to the water's edge. This time, I carried my own fly rod. It was much busier down here than where we'd been. As we passed behind the long line of fishermen, Fly Bob received a lot of waves and comments, like he was a superhero or something. Many fishermen knew and respected Bob's fishing knowledge and abilities, so it was kind of an honor to have Fly Bob as my own personal guide. I even saw Hal fishing downstream with Buff, the other guides. Junior was there again, also. Man, she knows where the good fishing is too, I thought.

"Welcome to combat fishing." Fly Bob bellowed. "A lot of people come up to Alaska and expect to have the water all to themselves only to find it's packed with fishermen! They go where the fish are. But hey, you're already broken in, so you'll be able to cast fine."

The fishermen stood almost shoulder to shoulder. Though intimidating, Fly Bob was right. I'd spent a lot of time casting and felt confident to fish alongside the Alaskans. I couldn't be called a cheechako now!

We waded into the water, with fish darting all around us, like we'd entered a flock of birds. Warm spots of ocean water mixed with the cold river and rushed by my waders.

I waited impatiently as Bob removed his fly box. What a mix of colors and patterns it contained, kind of like an artist's palette. Fly Bob performed his fly selection ritual, closing his eyes and running his palm over the flies in the box. It was almost like they were speaking to him, beckoning to come out. Then he opened his eyes, made his choice and pulled out a flashy looking fly.

"Let's try to find some slower pockets of water and find a stray pink that's willing to chase this Flash Fly."

Sure enough, Fly Bob spotted a back channel eddy that swirled and slowed the current. He knew how to read the water well anywhere he went in Alaska.

"Who's that, Bob?" One of the fishermen shouted.

"Don't you worry about it, Larry. This kid is going to out fish all of you today!"

Fly Bob whispered, "This is it," he insisted. "Cast there, then make quick strips of the fly and stop. Make sure you keep control of your line and stay in sync with the other fishermen around you."

He walked a little upstream and gave me some space to fish by myself.

All sorts of characters waded nearby and lined up for the chance to catch these chums. A woman in pink waders and sunglasses hooked into one. Then a guy with a camouflaged hat celebrated a catch. I also saw Junior with her rod bent. She was just a few anglers up from me and gave me a quick wave.

I took a deep breath, stepped into the fishing hole, and made a hasty roll cast into the eddy.

Strip the line...pause.

Strip the line...pause

Strip the line...zzzzzzzzzzzzzzzZZZZZZZZZZZZZZZZZZZZZz!

Fish off. I wasn't speedy enough.

I made a short cast out and then let the fly line sink and swing.

The line stopped, and I instinctively set the hook.

"Set a second time to be sure it's hooked," I heard Junior call.

I lifted again and felt a salmon pulsate through the rod. She was right.

"Fish on," I yelled.

That statement means a lot to Alaskans. Everyone reeled in and waited for me to bring in the fish.

I held on tightly as the humpy hooked itself, wiggled and took off. The hump on its back sliced through the water's surface like a shark's dorsal fin.

Over this summer I had learned to control the salmon's movements by turning the rod slowly from side to side. This smaller pink salmon was much easier to land as I stayed in sync with the fish's movements. Like the conductor of an orchestra, the fish moved in rhythm to my tempo.

I wanted to bring this fish in on my own. I moved the fish closer by working the rod and guiding him into shallower waters. I led the fish into my hands, and the pink gave one last shake and worked itself free of the fly.

"Quick release. Nice job, Pittsburgh," Junior commented and went back to casting. Somehow, she'd moved closer to the fishing spot next to me.

"Thanks."

"Doesn't count though," she muttered.

Sounds dumb, but I really wanted to get a picture of the pink for the slam. I worked even harder to catch the next one and finally brought in a pink.

I called Junior over to snap a picture of it for me.

"All you lower forthy-eighters come up here and want that perfect fish picture," she said. "If you're looking for perfect, you aren't going to find it in Alaska."

She snapped the picture on my phone.

"Hey, I didn't ask to come to Alaska for anything. I was forced to come." I replied.

"Well, guess we're both stuck here, then. At least you get to go home in a week."

I hadn't thought about the fact that we only had a little time left in Cooper Landing. I tried to take in all the scenery and decided to take a break.

I sat on the shoreline so I wouldn't lose my spot and pulled out a Lenny's and a Snicker bar. Junior eventually joined me. Luckily, I brought doubles of each.

"So what's your real name?" I covertly asked as I popped open a root beer and handed it to her.

"I'll never tell," she grinned as she took a gulp.

"Why Junior, then?"

"Do you want the long version or the short?"

"I guess the short."

"My dad wanted a boy to fish with, and he got me instead. After fishing with him all my life, kids around here started saying I fished as much as my dad, so the name Junior stuck. He left my mom and me when I was eight for another life. End of story."

Another Alaskan kid who had to be tough in a tough situation. It's harder when kids have to grow up quick. Guess everyone has a story behind the story in Alaska, not just me.

Junior got up and started casting again. She was into one before I'd even made a cast.

For another hour or so, we caught pink after pink. She shared a Bunny fly pattern with me, and we had a competition. After catching one, we'd display a fly angler's courtesy by handing the rod off to the other and moving out of the fishing hole. It became a silent contest with each of us trying harder to catch one quickly so we could hand off the rod with pride. Between the two of us, I estimate we caught over 20 humpies, though I can't really remember.

At least we were catching. It was always a good day when the fishing seemed more fun than the count.

"Catching is just a bonus," Dad would say at the beginning of all our fishing trips.

Today was a "bonus day," for sure.

Fly Bob returned after fishing for an hour upstream. "Well kid, looks like Junior taught you more than I did. You're a pro. I can't believe it. You're almost there to catchin' the slam."

I beamed a little with pride. Past the halfway mark to fulfilling my goal of catching the salmon five.

"Over the hump," I laughed.

Fly Bob and Junior laughed, too.

Only salmon anglers would get that joke.

My desire turned to determination. I now had only one week to catch two fish – a silver and a king. It didn't seem like such an impossible task now.

"Two fish to go."

I. ~~CHUM~~

II. ~~RED~~

III. KING

IV. SILVER

~~*V. PINK*~~

"The good news for you is I know a secret spot where the silvers should be running up the river later this week," Fly Bob said in a low whisper, as if he didn't want anyone around to hear.

"What about catching the king?"

I didn't think I had much of a chance catching a king since their run upstream was pretty much over for the summer.

"Well," said Bob. "Let's keep an eye and ear out for the beginning of the silver run and maybe we'll luck into that king."

If anyone could help me finish what I started, it was him.

"My arm's getting a little sore," I finally admitted.

Even Fly Bob showed some mental exhaustion.

"Ha," he replied. "I thought you were going to go for at least another hour."

I waved goodbye to Junior. Then Fly Bob and I waded back to the truck together, this time with him lagging behind. I glanced at the other anglers trying their luck and wondered if Hal and Buff had a bonus fishing day, too.

Just then, I heard a tremendous splash behind me. I turned to see only Fly Bob's head sticking out of the frigid water. My heart skipped a beat, and I was flooded of thoughts of Dad.

Luckily, Fly Bob had his wading belt cinched tightly, so his waders didn't fill with too much water. The current pulled him downstream a little ways, though.

I reached for him, but Fly Bob was too proud to receive any kind of help. He slowly worked his way from the crawling to the standing position and waved me along.

"Just got my foot stuck," he muttered. "I'll be OK." As Fly Bob took the next step, he winced, and an expression of pain came over his face. Closer to shore, I offered my help again. This time, he readily accepted and hobbled his way to the riverbank. I found a spot for Bob to sit down as he attempted to slide off his waders.

Fly Bob's right ankle had swollen so large so quickly that he couldn't take the waders off. Even through the waders, his ankle looked like an inflatable pool toy.

"Looks like I won't be fishing for a while," Fly Bob said feebly followed by some four-letter words. By the looks of it, I wasn't sure if Fly Bob could even get to the truck.

"I can't even pull them off," he said. "It's too swollen. Here, cut me out of these." Bob reached in his vest and handed me his silver fillet switchblade.

I flipped out the blade and began slicing Bob's waders from the top to the bottom of his boot. I put the knife in my vest pocket and helped Fly Bob work his leg, ankle, and foot free from the waders. Fly Bob let out a moan.

Buff and Hal worked their way up the path toward us.

"Are you tripping over those pinks again, Bob?" Buff shouted.

"Come on, Bob, you're supposed to catch them with your rod, not dive after 'em." Hal laughed.

"Ah, don't fool yourself. You're just coming over to see what flies I'm usin'." Even in a time of pain, Fly Bob kept his sense of humor and joked with his buddies.

Fly Bob rubbed his ankle and grrr'ed.

"Bob, don't think that you're gonna get out of guiding' for the rest of the summer," Hal scoffed with a grin.

"Yeah, the silvers are on the way, and we have too many clients to handle already."

"Come on, get me into my truck. I think I need to go to the clinic this time." Fly Bob groaned.

Junior and I exchanged worried looks.

Hal and Buff each got under one of Fly Bob's arms and assisted him back to the truck. Even though Fly Bob insisted on driving, Buff drove Fly Bob to the hospital while Hal took me and Junior along in his Jeep. I called Mom so she could meet us at the hospital clinic.

On the way, I leaned my head against the Jeep's passenger window and watched the scenery of Alaska pass by in a blur.

CHAPTER 14

July 20th — 8:04 a.m.

Dear Dad,

The good news is Fly Bob should recover by the end of summer. We stayed with him yesterday in the hospital until he got a cast on his broken ankle. The bad news is he won't be helping me catch the slam anymore.

Mom says she has a trip planned for us anyway, so I won't be able to fish. Still ten days until we leave, so not counting the slam out just yet.

Wonder what she has planned?

"OK, you're dressed in layers, right?" Mom asked.

"Yes," I reminded her. "You already asked me that." I patted my four levels of clothing and winter coat.

"I think I'm melting like a glacier underneath." I shared.

"Well, where we are going, you'll thank me later." Mom still didn't tell me where we were headed for the day, but I figured it was going to be cold.

"Will I at least be able to do some fishing toward the slam?" I inquired.

"Jack, I want you to set the Salmon Slam aside for one day. Would your dad want you obsessing over catching fish for him? You don't want to turn into Fly Bob, do you?"

I paused to think through those questions, but she didn't wait for me to answer.

"Your father would want you to embrace all of Alaska, not just the fishing. That's what we're going to do today. Something your father and I really wanted you to experience. Remember, he loved other things, too."

"OK, so what is it?" I asked.

She swung her ponytail in a happy way. "We're headed down to Seward to go kayaking near Kenai Fjord National Park. The ranger told me the orcas and seals were making their way into the bay, so maybe we'll see them today."

That sounded pretty cool.

I challenged. "Can I bring my fishing gear?"

She stared at me a while and finally said, "Fine."

We hopped in 'Ole Blue' since Fly Bob wasn't in any condition to drive and was taking a nap in the trailer with Salmo.

"You're in the way back this time, pal." Mom waved me toward the back of the pickup.

"What?" Then I saw Junior and her mom walking toward the truck with their gear.

"We have some guests joining us today," Mom smirked.

My stomach turned in river eddies.

"Since there's not a lot of room in the front, you guys can sit in the back. Just don't stand up while we're moving," Mom said.

Junior had her familiar wolf hoodie and a winter coat over it. She wore a purple knit cap like a skier would wear.

"Didn't know you could kayak," she taunted.

"We have water down in Pennsylvania, too," I replied coolly.

We jumped in the tail gate section and sat down, while Mom and Kim were in the cab. She drove us east on the Sterling Highway, and then headed south toward the quaint town of Seward. The wind slammed into us, so Junior and I huddled together against the back-cab window.

After about forty-five miles, we arrived in Seward. It was a salmon fishing town like Cooper Landing, but with more of a coastline feel since it was surrounded by the ocean. The wind really kicked up from the bay and left a chill in the air. The mountains, ocean, and ice seemed to meet here.

Mom led us to the docks where a barge-like boat stacked with kayaks sat among the other boats. Named the "Orca," its look and name reminded me of the boat in Jaws called 'The Orca.' Unfortunately, that boat had a disastrous ending I remembered.

"This is exciting, isn't it Jack?" Mom shared.

I nodded, not wanting to reveal my Jaw's plot thoughts.

The Orca barge gate dropped into place, and we walked on it. The captain was an older fellow with a prickly gray mustache and lanky figure named Captain Craig. His multitude of wrinkles showed that he'd taken this boat out on the water many times.

"Nice to meet you, I'm Cap." He shook all our hands. "The rain should hold off right past the bay, so I think we'll have decent weather to kayak to the glacier today."

It was only us four and Cap, so I'm sure Mom and Dad had paid a ton ahead of time for this private trip. I was just glad to have Kim and Junior along with us on the adventure. It somehow made it more special.

Puffin birds swooped over us as the boat pushed off the dock and motored toward the large rock cliffs in the distance. The snow-capped mountains surrounded the town of Seward and seemed close in on us. Conifer and Sitka trees sprouted from the mountainous cliff sites. I took pictures like crazy.

What an amazing place this was. I totally understood why Mom and Dad had planned this experience.

"Look at the seals over there," Kim said, pointing off to the left. A seal family lay lazily on a large ice chunk. As we got closer to the massive glacier in the distance, more and more seals and wildlife were active on the ice flows.

Man, the salmon have to make it past all these sea creatures and cold water to spawn.

The blueish glow in the distance exposed an enormous wall of ice. The glacier was the most enormous thing I think Mom and I had ever seen. Maybe the length of three football fields. We were headed right for it.

The Orca's captain steered the boat to a rocky shoreline on the left of the glacier. Then he dropped the front boat gate like we were a U-boat storming Normandy.

We walked off and helped unload the kayaks to shore. The captain gave us survival wet suits to put on, which were toasty. Then we placed life jackets over them. None of us planned on intentionally going into the icy waters.

Junior whispered, "In all my life, I've never kayaked here." She seemed nervous and didn't show her usual toughness.

I reassured her, "No worries, me either. We'll help each other."

Mom pushed off the shore in her kayak, and Kim followed. I went next, and Junior came in last, wobbling her way with zigzagging motions. The captain trailed behind; his job was to lead us closer to the glacier.

I put my hand in the frigid water. *How could marine life survive in this?*

Junior kept her kayak close to mine, and we paddled in sync toward the glacier for a while. I could tell she was a little unnerved by the kayak and icy waters. I showed her a few kayak tricks with the paddle, and she smiled with thanks. It felt good to finally show her something.

The massive glacier towered over us as we floated closer and closer. Only one lone boat motored near us, so we had the whole glacial bay to ourselves. The water was a sheet of icy glass and reflected the blueish tint of the wall.

Cracks and pops echoed through the valley of the glacier fissuring that sounded like a steam engine train gearing up to trek across the Alaskan plain. The pressure waves rattled in our bones with the thunder-like sound of the ice calving. Change was all around.

"Keep a look out for calving ice chunks to fall. Sometimes, they can cause big waves and disturbances for kayakers," The captain warned.

The weather near the glacier was like sticking my head in the freezer.

We lined our five kayaks together and stared at the massive ice wall.

"This is awesome," Junior called, and her voice echoed off the glacier. She seemed more confident now in her balance and ability to turn her kayak.

We all yelled different things at the wall.

Of course, I chose, "FISH-ON!"

Mom yelled, "You-whoooooo" in a melodic voice.

Kim shouted, "Salmon Chow-der!"

"Where we're floating now is where the glaciers used to be when I was little. This whole valley was filled with ice at one time." The captain shared.

Then he turned us back toward the boat to head back.

"Look off in the middle of the bay," he waved. "They're here, right on schedule."

I thought I saw a long dorsal fin sticking out of the water. Sure enough, three orca whales humped over out in the distance.

We paddled toward the disturbance in the middle of the glacial bay. The killer whales noticed our presence and turned in toward us. I have to say it wasn't the best feeling to be out in the open on kayaks. I felt like prey. The buzz of excitement was evident, even though no one made a sound.

Talk about wild, dangerous, and exciting at the same time.

One orca whale broke the surface, and I could see the black and white of its body. Its dorsal fin chopped through the water like a hot knife through butter.

Another orca turned and flashed its black and white body toward us. It seemed like they were playing with us.

"Just keep your kayaks still everyone," Cap ordered. We each stayed absolutely still while the pod of orcas swam around us and flopped about.

One came right below my kayak and surfaced with a spray of air coming out of its blowhole. I held my breath in excitement, and I could see Junior doing the same thing.

"These orcas are drawn to the salmon runs." Cap offered. "Sometimes, I can even recognize individuals by the shapes of their fins or the saddle patch behind their dorsal. I think this is a mom with her three babies."

I noticed one youngling had a grayish patch behind its dorsal and kept coming up for air.

The pod swam in a tight circle around us, then seemed to lose interest and took off towards the glacier.

Cap led us back to the boat, and we took in the sights.

'That was amazing, Cap!" Mom exclaimed.

"Well, in order to appreciate the killer whales, you gotta love the plankton that the little fish eat. Then you have to love the salmon that feed on those small fish. Then you can love the orcas," Cap said with a smile and a wink.

The salmon life cycle is vitally important from the tiniest creatures to the massive whales. On the way back to the dock, I realized that I hadn't thought about catching the slam all afternoon.

On the drive back, we stopped at a local dive restaurant north of Seward called the 'Moosequito Grill.' Cap had suggested we stop at this 'local watering hole' on the way to Cooper Landing.

What a different place this was from Gwin's since all the salmon angler regulars and natives stopped here. The buzz around the restaurant was centered on the salmon runs and upcoming weather. The smell of burnt pizza, fried fish, and alcohol engulfed the place.

Junior and I found it funny that couples were dancing in their waders while the jukebox played classic hits. She tried to get me out on the dance floor, but I didn't budge.

Mom bought matching 'Moosequito' hoodies and surprised us. They featured a big cartoon moose on the front.

"To remember your moose encounter, Jack!" Mom joked.

On Cap's suggestion, we all ordered the 'Moosequito' burger.

It was worth it.

CHAPTER 15

July 27th — 1:10 a.m.

Dear Dad,

Can't sleep. It's been raining here like crazy since we got back from the Kenai Fjords. All the rivers around the area are beyond the flood stage. Junior and I even took the whole day yesterday and fished from the shoreline. Not a king or salmon in sight.

So, I guess I won't be catching the Salmon Slam for you.

Mom won't let me go out in all this high water. She's afraid I'll drown. I'm sure the bears out there don't help my cause either, so the Salmon Slam ends here.

If you were here, I know we could finish it together. I'm sorry.

With heavy feet and slumped shoulders, I walked with Mom to the restaurant for breakfast. I'd felt similar anger toward her earlier in the summer, but this time I knew it was for my own good.

Can't blame Mom for this.

Alaska had defeated me. I know Mom said not to obsess, but with just a few days left, I'd come two fish short of the slam.

The restaurant was already buzzing with commotion when we entered. The waitresses poured coffee as Kim shuffled back and forth from the kitchen to the tables, taking orders, while the patrons feasted on their greasy breakfasts. Fly Bob waved to us from a stool where he was working hard at the grill, despite his cast.

I wasn't surprised to see Bob toiling in the kitchen and mixing up a fresh batch of salmon chowder in a large iron pot.

Hal sat in the corner eating breakfast and tying up some flies at his vise, and he waved Mom and me over.

"Hey man, check this fly out. I call it the Pink Pollywog," Hal said. "We call 'em 'Wogs' for short."

I watched as Hal layered in a bundle of dyed-pink deer hair on the hook shank.

'Wog,' a good name for a fly.

I knew it would float on the water since the deer hair was just like Dad's Elk Hair Caddis. This is what tiers do when the water is unfishable. They tie flies.

"Does it work? Will salmon really hit a dry fly?" I asked, furling my eyes in bewilderment.

Buff leaned over Hal's shoulder and butted into the conversation. "Let's just say this, Jack. The silvers will hit any fly, as long as it's pink!"

"Can't believe our clients bummed out and canceled the fly out trip. They woulda' had a great day on the water with those Wogs," Buff commented.

"So I'm thinkin' of flyin out to Bear Tooth Lagoon anyway," Hal shared. "Got my own Beaver, that's an airplane." He added for my clarification.

I pictured a big old beaver sitting in a lagoon somewhere.

"Should be some fresh silvers jumping when the tide comes in. Always gotta watch out for the bears, though, so it's good to have a bigger group. They're a little more aggressive at the lagoon. Usually, the more people the better to keep the bears at bay." Hal looked at me and Mom.

"We have the camp already set up with sleeping bags, tents, food, the works." Buff added. "All you need is your waders, rods, and warmer clothes. You two wanna go over night? I think Kim and Junior might come, too."

I glanced at Mom with a puppy dog look.

Please, please, please!

"Isn't the water too high everywhere to fish?" Mom pondered.

"Well, we figured we'd head west where they had less rain. Besides, it's an inlet, so the high water wouldn't matter as much," Hal answered.

After a little thought, Mom finally relinquished.

"OK, why not? I'd love to see Alaska again from the sky, and maybe I'll get more information for the book. One last adventure before we head back to the Burgh."

"Thanks Mom." I gave her a hug for reassurance on the decision.

The slam was back on!

"Think we can get Fly Bob to go?" I asked Hal.

"Well, let's put it this way...Bob hasn't gotten on a plane since I've known him. Even the lure of limiting out on silvers hasn't convinced him to step on my plane. Go try him, though. He might since you're going."

I strolled over to the counter, and Fly Bob hobbled over.

"What'll it be, partner? The salmon chowder is hot and fresh."

"Hal is flying me, Mom, Kim, and Junior on his plane to Bear Tooth Lagoon. Will you go with us? Please?"

I already knew the answer.

"Sorry Jack. You know me – a big ole' scaredy-cat to get on one of those death traps. Never have, never will."

I pressed harder.

"Come on..." I waited for the effect. "Do it for my dad."

He hesitated and barely whispered under his breath. "Sorry, I just can't do it."

I don't know why I said it, but it just blurted out. "You're nothing but a cheechako." I stormed away from him.

Fly Bob's body hunched over. He turned and limped back to the kitchen.

I wasn't going to let this stop me from trying for the silvers.

We headed back to the cabin to pack a few warm things and our fishing gear and met Hal and the others at the restaurant. We stuffed into the Jeep and drove to the little lake where Hal docked his plane.

Nicknamed the 'Fly Castor,' this plane was a seven passenger DHC-2 Beaver DE Havilland, single engine. On the doors, a cartoon beaver casted a fly rod. With bubble windows to see out of, it had pontoon floaters under it instead of wheels. I shot Mom a look of excitement, and she tried to hide her look of trepidation.

Hal handed us each a pair of ear plugs then pressed a few buttons, flipped some switches, and started the Fly Castor up like a pro. The propeller kicked off with a fury! Now, I understood why we needed to wear ear plugs. Buff sat up front and Mom, Kim, Junior, and I sat in the back on bench seats.

From the plane windows, I spotted a blue blur kicking up dust and driving on the road that led to the dock.

YES!

"STOP THE PLANE!" I hollered. "He's coming! HE'S COMING!" I tapped Hal on the shoulder to look.

Fly Bob hobbled out of Blue and onto his crutches. Salmo trotted behind. Hal opened the plane hatch and helped the man and his dog up into the cockpit.

"Hey Old Timer, this is a first!" Hal's eyes were open wide.

"This is only for my grandson," Fly Bob grumbled.

Then he winked at me. "Let's get this rust bucket airborne before I change my mind."

We all sat down and strapped in again. Hal and Buff in the front cockpit, and Fly Bob in the back with us. Salmo lay in between the front and back seats on the plane's floor. This was a normal trip for a dog in Alaska.

I smiled over at Fly Bob, but his eyes were closed.

Hal taxied down a strip of lake like a normal plane would head down the runway, 'Fly Castor' lifted into the air. It was a bumpy ride, but pretty smooth for such an old beaver plane.

Fly Bob gripped the seat cushion so hard that his hands turned white. They matched the whites of his eyes. I noticed Mom put her hand on Bob's shoulder. My hand squished against Junior's, but she didn't seem to mind, so I didn't move it.

Buff and Hal communicated through headsets as they'd done on this trip a million times.

Whitish-blue snow blanketed the mountain tops. What a spectacular view from above. The wilderness looked endless.

Hal swooped the plane around and lowered it in elevation. Bob's face turned even paler after the plane's tilt. My stomach felt the drop, too.

"I'm sorry," I mouthed over to Fly Bob.

"For your dad," he mouthed back and tried to smile weakly.

After only a fifteen-minute flight, we were ready to land in Bear Tooth Lagoon.

The beaver banked and descended toward the shoreline.

"Look down there," Hal encouraged in a crackly headphone sound, "you can see the outlines of all the silvers making their way around the lagoon."

We peered out of the weathered plane windows and saw silver salmon shadows clumped together on the edges of the banks. They resembled little minnows from this height and moved together like a flock of birds.

"What are those round brown dots on the edge of the water?" I yelled over the wind.

"That's why it's called 'Bear Tooth Lagoon.' Those are the bears," Junior smirked.

Mom clearly gulped, as I wrapped my mind around fishing with all those bears around us. Who better to be with than Hal, Buff, and Fly Bob, the three best fishing guides in Cooper Landing?

Hal drifted the plane into the middle of the lagoon and touched down. I watched as some bears scattered back into the wooded areas.

At least the plane scared them off.

My heart pounded with excitement when the plane landed on the water. Hal used a long stretch of the coastline to touch down landing smoothly on the water's surface. Like a beaver slapping its tail on the water, the 'Fly Castor' made a huge wave of water and came to a soft stop.

The color in Fly Bob's face slowly returned as he took in deep breaths. I took one, too.

So many firsts this Alaskan summer, and this was another big one.

Hal taxied to a makeshift dock before shutting all the buttons down.

"OK, let's catch some fish!" Hal said with a grin. "We just gotta stay clear of the big fellas. Watch out for Chewbacca. He's the aggressive 800-pound male that keeps chasing us out of these fishing holes! I'm sure we'll see Igor at some point, too."

I wrapped my head around how big an 800-pounder would be.

And who was Igor?

From our vantage point, we could see bears above us on the water's edge about a football field away. I noticed a large Grizzly Bear paw in the soft clay at the shoreline and piles of bear scat everywhere. They owned this island.

"As long as they're not on the move, we're safe." Hal reassured.

"Hey Bob, I'll take the first bear watch shift if you want to fish with Jill and Jack, then Buff can take the second shift," Hal announced. They sounded like guards chatting about controlling bear inmates in a wooded prison.

Still, the prospect of catching one of these amazing silvers offset my fear of the bears.

Fly Bob stayed on the shore while I waded in a little bit and Mom moved downstream. Buff, Kim, and Junior headed further down shore to give us the ideal silver fishing spot. By now, everyone knew how determined I was to catch the silver and didn't want to get in my way.

Fly Bob tied the Wog on my line. Tied with pink-dyed deer hair, it floated nicely on the water, like our bass flies at home.

"OK," said Fly Bob, settling into familiar territory on the shoreline. "This is sight fishing, totally different than what we've done before. Just pick an active fish who's feeding and move in on it. Try to dance that Wog along the top of the water. We're hoping they will take a chomp at it. The splashier you land the fly on the water, the better."

I tried the first cast and skated the fly too fast across the water's surface. With the first swing, I pulled the fly line in and waterlogged the pink Wog as it drifted under the water. I stripped in the line, blew on the fly to dry it, and made a second cast to the silvers. The water current made it difficult to keep the fly on the surface without dragging it downstream.

Junior already had one on with Buff down below. She waved up at me, but I pretended to ignore her and focused my attention in front of me.

"Be aware, these silvers like to make a few jumps like the rainbows." Bob shared. "If they do, be ready and bow down to give them a little line slack. That way, they won't break you off."

The second cast brought a silver to the surface, and it humped right over the Wog. I'd set the hook too late and felt the Coho roll off. Salmo barked at the prospect of seeing the fish come up.

"You gotta count one-two-three before you set the hook," Bob instructed. "Otherwise, you'll pull the Wog outta its mouth."

The third and fourth casts drew a few fish in, but none bit.

Off to the right of the pod, I saw one fish porpoising and made a good cast ahead of it. Then I worked the Wog back and forth, like a crippled insect or small mammal. The silver went after it and struck the surface. I waited for what seemed like forever, and then set the hook.

"Fish on!" I barked.

The silver exploded away from shore and made its first leap in the air, about three feet out of the water, with my pink fly still in its kyped-jaw. When it landed back in the water, the splash drew attention from everywhere. I could see birds circling above and the bears upstream take notice. Salmo ran back and forth on the shore.

"Get'em in quick, Jack. The bears just spotted an easy meal on the end of your line," Fly Bob warned.

I made the C-curve in my line and started working the silver into shore. I felt the fish surge through the rod as it made another leap in the air and bowed the rod down to leave some slack. Not as high this time, but still impressive.

Just then, an eagle came swooping down from the tops of the trees and buzzed right over my head. It was a massive brown and white streak with large talons and claws.

"That's probably Igor the Iggle. Right on cue. Better watch or he'll get your fish before you get 'em in." Fly Bob cautioned.

Igor swooped repeatedly to the surface of the water where my fish was making the commotion.

Fly Bob raised his crutches over his head and yelled. "Git bird, git!" Mom even got into the action and waved her hands back and forth like she was doing the wave.

Igor landed close to the water, managed to get his claws in my silver, and ripped it from the surface. My line snapped, and Igor dragged his salmon meal off into the trees.

"Ha ha. Igor wins again!" Hal joked. "He's done that to us more than once. Guess everybody needs to eat."

"Does that count toward the slam when an eagle steals it?" I asked with hope.

Fly Bob and Hal both gave me the thumbs-down.

"Gotta get him to the net," Fly Bob shared.

Luckily, Fly Bob had a lot of pink Wogs in his fly collection. He graciously gave me another to tie on. I retied some tippet line as quickly as I could and then attached the Wog.

I got a little sloppy with my cast in the wind, and it tangled on itself.

Fly Bob called me back to shore and helped me untangle the mess.

"Slow it down, Jack, you're trying too hard," he urged. "These Silvers like a good presentation. You can do this."

He handed me the rod and raised his hand for a high-five. I obliged and went back to my spot.

This was my best chance at catching the silver for the slam. I stayed laser-focused on my cast, presentation, and technique.

It's now or never, Cooper.

I made a few more casts, and finally, another silver took the wog. By this time, I'd had the experience of dodging bears, moose, and even eagles to hook my fourth salmon. I looked above me to monitor Igor, but there was no sign of him. He was probably still enjoying his fresh salmon meal, compliments of my last catch.

My rod bent further, and then the silver jumped as its scales glistened in the sunlight. I bowed to the fish before slowly working it back and forth within the currents.

When it turned, I turned. When it took off, I gave it slack.

Eventually, I could feel the silver tiring, and I reeled him closer to shore.

"Way to stick with it, man," Fly Bob beamed as he netted the fish.

"Great job, Jack!" Mom exclaimed, waving the others to come up.

"Why don't you all get in for a picture of this one?" Fly Bob said.

"Dude, are you kidding? You need to be in this pic, too," Buff suggested.

Buff stood knee deep in the water, and we all got on shore around Fly Bob with me in the front.

Surrounded by Fly Bob, Mom, Junior, Kim, Hal, and Salmo, I hoisted the enormous salmon in front of us.

Buff called out, "The Kenai Kids, Part Two," and I thought back to the photo at Gwin's.

Buff snapped the pic of the silver.

I was one salmon closer to finishing the slam.

I. CHUM

II. RED

III. KING

~~*IV. SILVER*~~

~~*V. PINK*~~

With Fly Bob's instruction, even Mom caught a few silvers while I took a break and watched for bear activity.

By the end of the afternoon, we had all caught our limit of silvers and had sore shoulders to prove it.

Buff had a campfire going as the evening approached and cooked up some of the silvers we'd caught that day. They also had different types of chips, salads, and cookies, like a buffet on the edge of the water. The guides really treated their fishing clients in style. I thought the food would attract bears, but it stayed quiet.

After dinner and sharing who caught more, Mom and Junior helped set up the tents while I helped Hal and Buff rid the camp of any leftover food. Fly Bob and Kim filleted the rest of the salmon to take back to camp in freezer bags.

"These bears can smell anything left out and will come for it," Hal warned. "Don't even leave a crumb. The Alaskan ole' timers call this 'cache-ing.'" That explained why I was seeing signs all over the place with that word.

The guys were prepared, as they had food bags and coolers to keep the salmon and food smells contained.

"Well guys, this was an amazing day. Thanks for including us on the adventure. I'm really tired. Think I'll head to the tent." Mom said.

"Night Mom," I responded, giving her a big bear hug.

The sun held on low in the sky, and the night air started to cool off and move us closer to the campfire. I could hear wolves howling, communicating to each other off in the distance.

A little later, it was Kim's turn to head to bed.

That left the rest of us sitting and staring into the fire as embers flew high into the Alaskan sky.

"Hey Bob," Hal blurted. "Tell the kid 'The Legend of the Soul-less

King.' That's one of my favorites."

"He doesn't want to hear anymore salmon legends. Ace tells him enough already," Bob mumbled.

"Yeah, yeah, I do want to hear it." I insisted.

"Nah, your mom wouldn't appreciate me scarin' you," Fly Bob responded.

I begged again. "Please? Can you tell it?"

"It's about drowning, Jack. It's about drowning," Fly Bob admitted.

"I can deal with it, really, I can."

The campfire flickered shadows in Fly Bob's beard. He nodded and began the tale.

"OK, well...legend around these parts is there's one salmon, a King salmon, who swims in from the ocean each year. He finds the deepest part of the river and swims in plain sight. He's not scared of any man, bird, bear, or beast since he's the largest creature in the sea, a king and ruler of all. This massive salmon isn't here to spawn. He has another more sinister purpose: to take the souls of the foolish and the arrogant. Men, women and even children are lured into the deep water not only by his beauty and size, but by his power."

Fly Bob used a long stick to draw circles in the dirt in front of him.

"Each time an angler makes a cast to him, he entices them further and further into the river. To catch him, they keep stepping closer and closer. *'One more cast,'* they say, *'just one more.'* He slowly leads them into the current until they lose their footing..."

At this, Fly Bob cracked the stick, and I flinched.

"...and are swept away by the powerful Kenai River never to be seen again."

The story was all too real. I imagined Dad being swept into the currents for the fiftieth time. I stood and walked away from the fire.

"Sorry for suggesting that," Hal whispered. "Guess it's too close to home for a kid who's just lost his dad."

I came back and faced the fire. "I'm going to catch a King for Dad and finish the slam," I declared.

Silence permeated the air around the campfire.

"I think you're going to do it," Fly Bob said softly.

Buff responded a little louder, "Dude, I don't mean to break any bubbles here, but there's really not much of a chance now that the kings have spawned and become fish food."

"Yeah" Hal admitted, "you probably have a one in a hundred chance to get one since they're all spawned out. Just not many out there to catch. Besides, the water levels are way too high with all the rain in the forecast the next few days."

"Give the kid a break," Fly Bob interrupted. "I've caught kings into August before. He still has a chance to get one. That's all he needs, just one."

With that, everyone milled around before heading to their respective tents for the night. I think they sensed what I feared – *catching a King to finish the slam was an impossible task.*

"I'll stay up with the fire tonight guys, sleep tight," Fly Bob volunteered. "We'll be safe from the bears with the fire, no worries."

"OK Bob, I'll see you around threeish to take over." Buff offered.

Junior walked by and punched me lightly in the arm. "Hey Pittsburgh, four outta five ain't too bad. I'm goin' to bed, night guys."

The fire crackled as we stared into it. Fly Bob reached over and put his hand on my shoulder.

"Hey Jack-O...just one," he whispered. "Just one."

Just one.

CHAPTER 16

ALASKAN ☆
FACTS:

The King Salmon (Chinook) is the
Alaskan State Fish.
It grows from 20 to 90 pounds and
measures between 30 to 55 inches.

July 29th — 6:28 a.m.

Dear Dad,

This is it, last chance to finish the slam. We're leaving tomorrow.

It's a freezing cold morning and has been raining buckets every day since we got back from Bear Tooth. The rivers are still running high.

But I can't stop now. Mom and Fly Bob don't know I'm going out to fish today. They would say the water's too dangerous and probably not let me go. So I'm off early.

I may not catch the slam for you, but at least I'm trying.

I must at least try.

The clouds hanging around the mountains cemented the valley's deep cracks. The weather would sit upon Cooper Landing all day like this. My last day to fish.

Just like a salmon spawns only once, I had one more chance to catch the last fish of the slam.

I'll be OK.

An Alaskan Railroad train couldn't have stopped me from fishing and drowning was not on my to-do list.

The camp seemed deserted. Even the animals remained in bed just a little longer. I hoped Salmo would come along as usual, but even she decided it was too chilly and stayed inside.

I hurried past Fly Bob's trailer, but a faint whistle got my attention. He waved me inside.

"OK, young man, I know I'm not going to convince you not to go fishing today. You've got that stubborn Cooper blood in you. Come on in. I tied you up one of my best flies."

Inside the warmth of his trailer, Fly Bob removed a sparkling fly from his vice. Tied on a number four hook, the marabou feather on its end undulated as Bob swam it through the air.

"That's called the Alaskan Express," he boasted.

It seemed like another streamer pattern, like the Woolly Bugger I tied with Dad back home only with some minor differences. Definitely much longer and bigger.

First, Fly Bob tied it with a purple chenille and flashy material in the tail. Then he tied what looked like a pink egg in front of it.

"That fly simulates a leech sucking on a salmon egg. The salmon go nuts for it. You're going to need it in this fast and murky water. Only a big strong King will go after this one. A royal fly fit for a King."

The sun's muted rays found their way through the cracks into the trailer. I held up the Alaskan Express in the dim light. It seemed to be two flies in one – a bugger and an egg fly.

"Thanks."

"I don't need to remind you to..." Fly Bob stopped mid-sentence with a little trepidation in his face.

He quickly changed the subject. "You have your bear spray with you, right?"

I nodded.

"Ah, who am I kidding? You know what you're doing now, kiddo.

Those bears should be afraid of you. You got your wading belt on tight, right?" Fly Bob checked my belt and tightened it up a notch. "You watch yourself out in that current today. Go catch that King!" Fly Bob smiled.

I petted Salmo and headed out of the trailer.

"Hey Jack, wait a minute, you might need this..." Fly Bob hobbled over to his fishing gear and fumbled through it.

He pulled out his favorite 10-foot 10 weight fly rod, the Excalibur, and traded rods with me.

"Here, for the fast water today. The reel has a sinking tip line that's a little heavier. Just don't lose it!"

"Wow, thanks," I bear hugged Fly Bob. Not just a regular hug, but one that's for a family member.

"I'll protect it with my life," I promised.

"OK, you got two hours before I call the cavalry in for you and let your mom know where you are. I'm sending Salmo with you, too. Keep calm and fish on, young man."

I gave him a salute and headed off. Salmo walked with me, tail wagging. I hiked to the same trail Fly Bob and I took on my first days in Alaska. I planned to hike down to the Chutes and Ladders falls where Dad had fished when he was my age and work my way down.

Maybe that place would be lucky for another Cooper boy.

The familiar and ominous sign on the way to the trailhead froze me in my tracks:

> **ALWAYS**
> **HAVE A BUDDY**
> **IN BEAR COUNTRY!**

It had much more meaning now that I was alone. At least Salmo was with me. She seemed to smile when I looked down at her.

Further up the trail, I arrived at the cottonwood gates. I couldn't hide a growing smile and bowed to each of the trees, paying a magical respect to the Alaskan woods and all it held. I thanked the wilderness for all it provided this summer.

No longer an immature jack salmon that arrived early in the summer.

No longer the Cheechako from the lower forty-eight.

No longer like the 'Salmon Boy.' I had respect for my surroundings, the weather, and especially the wildlife.

I'm ready for this.

I passed into the thicker bush along the trail, and the cold drizzle soaked through to my bones. Still, I paused when reaching the limestone spring to fill up my canteen. Salmo took a few licks as well. Staying hydrated even in the rainy weather was important, and I wanted to dedicate the entire day to fishing.

An immense crack sounded in the woods, grabbing my attention. Something was close. The question was who or what? Controlling my breathing, I listened for signs of movement. The absence of chirping birds indicated a large animal, possibly a bear or a moose, was nearby. The creature had paused to listen as well. Salmo's hair bristled as she sensed something, too.

After a few minutes of silent standoff, I pressed on to the water. Soon I'd be on the narrow path downward to reach the river, a much better vantage point for me.

Reaching the pathway without incident, I turned downhill to the river. Fly Bob's voice echoed in my head, reminding me to watch my every step down the path. Dad's voice echoed too, encouraging me to appreciate the beauty around.

I'm not alone.

I reached the river's edge and saw the water cascading in a fury. It was much higher and faster than I expected. Realization set in.

Catching a King here would be harder than climbing Denali in the dead of winter.

I walked past the shadowy water looking for signs of fish. Pods of fish made their way upstream, but the cast across the river would be too difficult. Fly Bob had reminded me to use my body to get into the best position not only to hook the fish but land it as well.

Wading further downstream, I searched through the "windows" looking for salmon. Between sections of turbulent white water, I scanned the river with patience and focus. The old Jack would have rushed into the water and began fishing; but here, observing the water first made an angler more successful. I wished Dad could've been with me now to see how far I'd come as a fisherman and outdoorsman.

Then I saw it; this was the spot to start. The river opened down here which lowered the water to wading levels.

Tough wading, but manageable.

Standing over a long flat section of water, I witnessed commotion in the stream behind some large rocks. Salmo came to my side and sat. A mammoth fish jockeyed for position behind a huge boulder. The fish looked like a Volkswagen bug had parked itself in the middle of the river. OK, maybe not that big, but it was the biggest fish I had seen this summer. Its size and black gums revealed what type of fish it was. The boulder was a great place for a King to take a break from the current.

I scanned the woods for a large stick. Fly Bob taught me to utilize what nature had provided. I found a solid branch to serve as a great wading staff and brace against the strong currents.

I knew Mom would be mad. Fly Bob would never try a stunt like this with the high water; but then again, Fly Bob wasn't as desperate as me to catch a King.

With great risks come great rewards. With that thought, I forged into the icy water.

Don't be stupid, Cooper. Baby steps.

You never get used to that first step into frigid waters. My body tensed like an iron rod as the chills gripped me. I gasped as my body temperature adjusted.

Salmo paced back and forth on the shoreline. Even she didn't want into come in the river.

I made my way out to the boulder as the rocks beneath my feet sank deeper and deeper. Soon, I was nearly up to my chest with only a few inches of clearance before water would spill into my waders. I had to step slowly and carefully, or I'd be downstream in a hurry. I'd seriously underestimated the depth of the water this time, but since I'd made it this far, I decided to take some casts.

With minuscule steps, I shuffled forward so as to not lose balance. The water rushed by in a fury, but I remained calm and determined to reach the casting spot. After five minutes and only ten feet further, I was in position to cast to the dead water spot behind the boulder and hook that fish. My plan was to slowly make my way backwards to beach it on land. My exit strategy was in place.

From the rod's eyelets, I unhooked Fly Bob's creation. If anything would catch a King today, the Alaskan Express would be it.

The water pounded against my waders over and over, but I held firm, my feet spread and planted within the ground, my stick firm against the current.

Don't cross your feet.

I swung the line around and upstream so that it plopped in right behind the boulder. From the corner of my eye, I saw the impressive fish clearly now in the fishing window. Keeping a drag-free drift would be nearly impossible with the force of the water around it.

I made five or six more casts before shuffling my feet a little closer. Dad said changing the smallest things made the biggest difference in fishing: the cast, position, speed, depth, movement. I took baby steps closer, and even though my brain told me to stop, my feet didn't.

The water was up to my chest now and only an inch from the top of my waders. I could feel the frigid water through my waders. This was much different than standing in waist high water in a lake.

Just as I swung out a cast, an enormous shadow appeared in the water gliding on the outside edge of the slack behind the boulder. The shape drifted back and forth easily between the two.

I drifted my line downstream and then used the current to swing a cast back upstream. The fly landed right above the shape.

The Alaskan Express swirled between the two currents in line to bump the shadow right on its nose before slowly making its way downstream, and I waited with anticipation to see what the fish would do.

Suddenly, the shadow took the opportunity, turned its head into the slack water and opened its enormous kyped-mouth. It ripped the fly from the current and headed into the slack water. I set the hook firmly. The fish had taken the fly, but it didn't even notice it.

I braced myself and yanked the rod straight up in the air with my arms raised. Then I bore the fury of the fish on the end of my line.

This is a big one!

Just then, I gave one more hook set to be sure the fly was in the jaw of the beast.

Once the fish realized it had a hook in its mouth, it darted around the boulder and upstream. It knocked me a little off balance, and my right foot wedged under one of the boulders.

The fish continued to rip line off my reel faster than I'd ever experienced, but now I had other things to worry about. My position in the current allowed the frigid waters to rush into my waders, and the suction of the waders pulled me under.

I couldn't regain balance, and water kept coming and coming, pushing me further backwards. Now the water rushed over my shoulders and even splashed up to my neck. I had to do something fast or the current would take me. Mom couldn't lose her son the same way her husband died. Somehow, I had to get unstuck from the boulder.

I'd have to go all the way under to release my foot. Memories of my bad dream entered my mind. Adrenaline pumped through my body and woke me up.

I have to do something, NOW!

Stay calm.

I dropped down in the water.

Don't let go of his rod, even if it means you have to drown!

In a weird way, the underwater currents seemed less chaotic and peaceful. After opening my eyes and feeling around, I saw my boot was sandwiched between a crevasse of rocks. I came back up for a breath of air to try and figure out how to get out of this predicament. The cold water pierced my skull like millions of needles.

Keep calm, Cooper.

When I stiffened to a straightened position, I was submerged deeper and couldn't reach the surface for air.

Now panic gripped me from the inside.

I can die here.

My heart pounded. I needed air.

Think Jack, think!

I squeezed the rod handle hoping for an idea. I concentrated all my energy trying to dislodge my stuck leg.

No use, the boulder wasn't letting go.

Now the water flowed over my head.

Closing my eyes, I relaxed my body. The river currents swayed me back and forth like underwater grass. The darkness engulfed me. Exhausted and worn down, I gripped my body tight as the cold began to overtake me.

Thoughts took me to times with my father, on our favorite stream, and the many times we waded and fished together. I thought of how much I loved Mom, and the incredible summer we'd spent together in Alaska. Then I pictured Fly Bob – standing in his waders, smiling, and gripping a salmon high in the air. It was as if all my loved ones were giving me a final underwater embrace. The last bubbles of air left.

I squeezed my arms closer to my body and felt something stick out from Dad's vest.

Fly Bob's knife!

Cut yourself free.

I awoke from the daze and sprang into action to rip the knife out. I moved in slow motion but knew I had only seconds before I would lose consciousness. Guiding the knife blade down my leg to my boot, I tore the boot's laces with the knife point.

An intense burning began in my chest commanding my body to gasp for air.

Just hold on a little longer.

I sensed a little wiggle room and worked my foot out of the wading boot. Just then, the salmon still attached to the line, lurched downstream on the rod, giving me the extra tug I needed to pull free from the boot.

I splashed for the surface and reached out with my mouth like a fish gasping for air. After gulping oxygen and a little water, I began free falling down the middle of the river, tumbling with the rod in hand.

Now what?

Keeping my head above water, I coughed and breathed while trying to keep my balance within the current. I sped downstream with the rushing currents, like a pinball bouncing with no direction.

'Keep your legs forward,' I recalled Fly Bob instructing if I ever fell into the currents.

As the icy river dragged me further and further downstream, my body became numb and stopped responding to my brain.

I only had a few minutes to swim out of the frigid water or risk dying from hypothermia or drowning. I tried working my body over to the shoreline, but it was no use; exhaustion had set in. I could hear Salmo barking, but I couldn't spot her on the shoreline.

The King made a surge, and I felt the rod jerk forward. My forearm tingled with pain.

I searched the shoreline and finally recognized where I was on the river. It was the first place Fly Bob had taken me, the Spruce Tree Hole. I spotted an overhanging tree branch and knew it was my only chance to climb out of the river.

I rushed faster and faster towards the tree. The currents slammed me right into the bough of the tree, which hung into the water. Pain seized through my back. Even though it was excruciating, I knew it was a good sign that I still had feelings in my nerves. I managed to hold my head above water while the currents pummeled me.

Using my free arm, I struggled to pull myself along the limb closer to shore. Slowly, I straddled the bough out of the rushing currents. My skin scraped along the coarse branch, and blood poured from my arm. The burning pain left my extremities fast. I finally pulled myself to slower moving and shallower water while still gripping the rod.

The cold seized through my torso, and my legs ached with pain. I dropped limp on the rocky shoreline, and it took all my strength to hold onto Fly Bob's rod. Surprisingly, the fish remained securely fastened and pulsated on the line.

As I tried to get myself to a standing position, my body shivered uncontrollably. My joints throbbed and tightened against my will, like the Tin Man in the Wizard of Oz.

Focus, just get this fish in.

Reel, reel, reel.

Although out of the water, the wetness inside my shirt and waders made the outside air feel even colder. My teeth chattered, and it took every ounce of effort for me to turn the reel handle. The fish kept tension downstream and pulled like a bus hooked on the end of my line.

At times, I could sense the tug of the fish, then he'd let go. I wondered if the fish were still on my line.

I dipped my rod downward, and this time I felt the fish for sure. I reeled in inch by inch to bring the salmon upstream as he jerked back and forth.

One of the guides had mentioned that Kings fight one minute per pound. If this fish were over twenty pounds, he'd still have ten minutes of fight left.

How much fight do I have left in me?

The massive king gave a last burst of energy and dug itself deep on the river's bottom. My arms went noodle-limp, and I almost lost my grip. Regaining my balance, I fought the urge to let go.

Barking hysterically, Salmo had finally made her way down on the other side of the river.

"Easy gal," I called. "I'm OK!"

Salmo stood on the shoreline waiting for me to somehow make my way back over.

Working my rod from side to side with both hands, I moved the king from its hiding spot and brought it across the current. The mammoth began to tire out, making it easier to reel into shore.

I orchestrated like a maestro as the Alaskan wind taunted me to catch the final fish of the slam. The rain picked up and poured down buckets from the sky. I bellowed over the teeming rain.

"FISH ON!!!" I screamed as loud as I could muster.

"FISH ON!!!" My voice echoed over the rain through the valley.

By now the fish swam only twenty yards away. I caught a better glance. Its shadowy shape remained near the darkened river bottom.

Finally, the king rolled over on its side and gave in, but I didn't have much energy or even fly line left on my reel. I tugged the rod back to work the fish into the shallow rocks, but he still had a little water left to surge away. I set the rod down on shore and crawled my way over to the beached king. On my knees, I came face to face with its kyped-jaw opening and closing in the shallow water.

I laid face down on the rocks as another wave of exhaustion swept over me.

No one but me would ever see the last fish of the slam. I wished Fly Bob was here. I wished Mom was here. I wished Dad could've been here.

"This...one's...for...you...Dad," I mumbled.

Just then, out of the corner of my eye, I spotted someone in waders walking toward me. I turned my head and saw a figure lean over and pick up the King salmon.

Working myself up to a sitting position, I saw what looked like Dad standing over me holding the massive king.

"Is this a dream...or am I dead?!?" I asked.

"I'm proud of you, Jack," Dad whispered. "You did it."

Dad unhooked the Alaskan Express from the king's kype and set the fish down into the water. He worked the fish back into the water currents with his gentle, rugged hands, just as he'd revived many fish before.

I studied his smile and looked into his big, green eyes.

Was this real?

My father held the king under the belly with one hand, gripped the tail with the other, and the king quickly regained its energy. It surged upstream, made a mighty flop with its tail, and headed into deeper water.

Water splashed my face, and I slowly opened my eyes.

Had I been dreaming?

I stared at the low clouds and tree branches above before realizing I was lying down again. I sat up, looked around, and realized Dad was nowhere in sight. I reached over for the king, and it was gone, too.

My brain was fuzzy as I tried to wrap my mind around everything that happened.

Where was I and what was I here for?

I still held Fly Bob's rod in my hand, and the knife lay on the rocks nearby. My fly line and fly sat coiled in the gravel. Shivering, waves of extreme sleepiness crashed on my eyelids.

Stay awake!

I heard barks.

Stay awake.

But exhaustion took over, and my eyes rolled back.

I laid back down on the rocky surface.

Love you, Dad.

CHAPTER 17

ALASKAN ☆
FACTS:

☆ ☆ ☆
☆ ☆
☆ ☆
☆

**The State Flower of Alaska is the
'Forget-Me-Not.'**

July 30th — 2:02 p.m.

Hi Dad,

My hands are too sore to even write, but I just had to. I'm writing to you from a hospital clinic somewhere outside of Cooper Landing.

Can you believe that they brought a helicopter in to rescue me from the river, and I don't even remember it??? How cool is that? A helicopter!

I guess I went into hypothermic shock, and the Alaska State Troopers got to me in time. They lifted me out of the river valley and took me here to the clinic. I have an IV in my arm to get some fluids back, but I'm still feeling a little groggy. At least Mom brought my journal here.

She isn't so happy with me, but I know she's glad I'm still alive. I probably scared her beyond belief. The nurse said she slept in a chair in my room all night. She probably thought the Salmon People took me forever.

Funny thing, the hospital has 'Forget-Me-Not' flowers in all the rooms.

I'll never forget you, Dad. Thanks for being there with me for the slam.

I. CHUM

II. RED

III. KING

IV. SILVER

V. PINK

As I crossed out the last salmon in my journal, Fly Bob hobbled into the room.

"Look who's up?"

I closed my journal and strained a grin.

My muscles ached, and my arms were tight.

"How you feelin', Champ?"

"Like I was hit by an Alaskan train."

"Yeah, you're not supposed to fall in. Those waters'll do that to ya. I fell in once, and it took me three days to warm-up. But you're a young'en, your body will recover faster than an old guy."

"Where's Salmo, is she OK?" I worried.

"Yeah, she's sleeping back at the trailer. She had the ride of her life with you in the helicopter. Good thing she was there; she barked like crazy when the rangers tried to find you!"

Fly Bob pointed to his rod leaning over by the door, "But hey, I see you held onto the Excalibur! Guess it's yours now."

"Really? But it's yours."

"That rod is a part of your Alaskan story, now. Besides, you need your own salmon rod if you're going to fish with me next summer."

I really grinned now.

"I have a little something else to cheer you up. We'll meet at Gwin's tonight for your last Alaskan dinner. I've got you a going away present."

"I'm next," Mom said, peeking over Fly Bob's shoulder from the doorway.

"Mom!" I hugged her like I never had before.

"I'm sorry I went out Mom, but I had to…"

"Shhh..." She buried my head in her shoulder. "You have too much of your father in you, that's what worries me. I'm so angry at you! But you know what, I'm proud of you, too. You did a great thing for your dad this summer. Right now, I'm just thankful you're okay and in one piece!"

"No worries, Mom...I'm done fishing in high water." I looked over Mom's shoulder at Fly Bob wearing his usual camo jacket and Pirates hat. We winked at each other.

"Yeah right!" She scoffed. "I know you too well. I think you just wanted to stretch this trip out another day."

"Oh yeah, weren't we supposed to head up to Anchorage today?" I asked.

"I extended our stay and moved our plane flights by a day. You're welcome," Mom replied with a smile.

"Somebody else came with us to see you, too..." Fly Bob chimed in.

"Hey Pittsburgh," was all Junior said with a wave. This time she wasn't wearing a hat or waders. Her dark hair curled down over her Moosequito hoodie.

Mom grinned, put her arm around Fly Bob, and they both strolled out of the room.

Junior peaked at the door window like she was going to steal a bed pan or something. Then, she walked to my bedside and said, "You're such a dummy," before planting a kiss on my cheek.

"My real name is Everly," she shared.

I didn't mind the kiss, which surprised even me.

Kim barged in next with a cartload of food – fresh hoagies, chips, and cookies from the lodge.

"Ready to eat something?" She asked, and I didn't wait for anyone else before grabbing at the food.

Mom, Fly Bob, Junior, Kim, the nurses, and I chowed over lunch while I shared my adventure of catching the last salmon of the slam.

After I had a few fluids in me and my body got to a normal temperature, the hospital released me that afternoon. Back at the cabin, Mom and I spent the rest of the evening packing a summer's worth of clothes, supplies, and souvenirs into our duffel bags. It was going to be tough saying goodbye to Cooper Landing and everyone. Weirdly, I felt the same way packing to go back home as I had before I came to Alaska. I didn't want to leave.

The whole gang was going to meet us at Gwin's Lodge for a last supper of sorts, and it seemed like a good way to end our trip.

Mom held my hand as we made the quick walk over.

When we walked in, the whole restaurant yelled, "FISH ON!"

Everyone was there – Hal, Buff, Fly Bob, Gill, Ace, Kim, Junior, and a lot more people, even the restaurant's owners. Some of the park rangers and the Alaskan Troopers who saved me, including Ranger Rick, stood in the background. Even Corhyn and Cap came.

Fly Bob stood with his fishing pack and waved me over. "Come on over, Mr. Fisherman. This night is for you."

As I stood in front of everyone, he pulled out a rectangular shaped piece of cardboard.

"All your friends at the Lodge and me made somethin' for ya. Thought you needed some kinda reward for catching the Slam."

Fly Bob had traced his large hand in black Sharpie on an oversized piece of brown cardboard. On each finger, the names of salmon were written, and the flies were poked into the cardboard, too.

"The fingers are the salmon you caught, and those are the flies you got 'em with. Somethin' to take back to Pennsylvania to remember the Salmon Slam."

Everyone clapped and cheered.

I chuckled. *Only a rag-tag bunch of Alaskan guides would make something like this.* I pictured them sitting in the restaurant creating this work of art like

Alaskan kindergarteners at craft time. But I cherished it more than anything.

As I read each finger, CHUM, RED, KING, SILVER, PINK, I recalled all the flies which Bob had hand tied. Fly Bob was right. Just like the rod, each one held a story. Each one caught a salmon. They were now a part of my story, my journey.

"Congrats, young man. It's not easy to catch the slam in one summer, and you did it for your dad. Well done!" Fly Bob praised, patting me on the back.

"But how did you know I caught the King?" I asked.

"Well, we fisherman have tricks of the trade. When I took the Alaskan Express fly off your line, a big ole' King scale was on the end of it. I figured you danced with an ogre!"

"That I did. Thanks," I said. "But, I couldn't have done it without you." I got a little choked up.

Fly Bob leaned over and gave me his usual smelly bear hug.

"Remember Jack," he shared, "even though your dad is gone, part of him will always be with you. Think of the salmon life cycle: their strength, instincts, and their drive all come because they have the power of their parents before them, like you do. Salmon Strong!"

"Salmon Strong!" I replied.

Mom held back some happy tears.

"Now for the main course!" Kim shouted.

The spread was a whole buffet including Gwin's Lodge favorites like mini Moose Burgers, Salmon Chowder, Salmon patties, and of course, Gwin's specialty and Dad's favorite, the Halibut Burger.

I talked with the park rangers and troopers for a while and thanked them for their help in getting me back. They joked that they'd be less busy with me gone.

Then Junior walked over and handed me a Lenny's. "Come on, Pittsburgh. Think we could just let you leave without saying goodbye one last time?"

"Thanks Alaska," I laughed as I raised my bottle to hers.

Junior and I shared the sendoff as I gave her Dad's camo hat, and she returned the gift with her wolf hoodie.

I reminisced and thanked everyone who helped make the Salmon Slam possible this summer.

We all shared a summer's worth of salmon stories on my last evening in Alaska.

EPILOGUE

RIPPLES

The UPS package arrived at our house right on time, and Mom brought in the huge box.

"Well, here we go..." She held her breath, cut the box lid open, and pulled out a single book from the top of the pile.

The glossy cover revealed a large salmon background and the words "Salmon Slam: The Alaskan Guide to Fly Fishing for Salmon: By Redds, Jillian, & Jack Cooper. Foreword by Fly Bob."

"Wow Mom, you did it! Dad would be proud!" I gave her the appropriate bear hug.

"Yeah, we did it!" She said, smiling through joyful tears.

We celebrated by defrosting some of Fly Bob's salmon chowder. Mom had kept it frozen for this special occasion. Then she pulled out some glasses with the blue Alaskan flag on them.

"Remember these souvenirs?" She asked.

I'd forgotten she bought souvenirs on the train ride.

"Wait! I have something to toast with," I said. I ran down to the basement fridge and pulled out the last two Lenny's 'Laskan Root Beers.

I'd been saving them for a special occasion, too.

No better time than this.

When Mom saw them, she grinned, "Perfect, Jack!"

I filled our Alaskan glasses and watched as the root beer fizz bubbled behind the Alaskan flag.

"A toast to your father..." Mom said.

"...and to Fly Bob," I added as I raised my glass high.

"To Alaska," Mom said.

"And Benny," I responded.

Then we clinked glasses.

"I couldn't have finished it without you, Jack! Take a look at the Foreword. It was a secret gift from Fly Bob to you."

While I sipped my chowder, Mom pulled out a black felt tip pen and added her signature to the title page.

"To Jack – What an adventure with you! I love you forever."

I wanted to give Mom some time to chat about the book on the phone with her friends, so I chugged my root beer, grabbed my book copy, and headed to the shed. I slid the book into my fishing sling pack along with a fly box and my rod, in case the fish were biting. The water at the stream might be just about right for a few trout willing to take an offering.

As I hurried down the path, I realized the last time I'd been here was last summer before I left on the Alaskan trip. So many things had changed since then, but the path remained as familiar as always. Though still early April, new fern growth sprouted along the trail; squirrels hopped from tree to tree, and the water raged louder as I moved closer to the stream.

After a brisk walk down, I arrived at the stream and sat on Table Rock. It was tough, but I set the fly rod aside, because I couldn't resist looking at the finished book, especially Fly Bob's words. He'd never mentioned he could write. I opened the front cover and flipped a few pages to reveal his surprising foreword:

FOREWORD

There are few things in this world that are worth counting on – the sun to rise, the seasons to come and go, a family member to love, and a salmon run to begin.

When salmon begin their life's journey, they are bright, shiny, and untouched. Then they head out to the ocean to eat and grow. Finally, they return home to spawn. In this process, they are chased, bitten, bruised, beaten-up, scarred and often eaten. But in the end, some of them make it to spawn and begin anew, and the salmon life cycle continues.

I began fly fishing over thirty years ago with my son, John, who we later nicknamed Redds. He was a natural with casting, loved the water, and was obsessed with fishing. He loved flipping over rocks and locating samples to take back to the tying bench. At night, we'd tie up versions to match those critters and set them on the lamp shade to dry. Redds couldn't wait to get up the next morning to test them out in the streams. When Redds experienced the waters of Alaska, he found his gift. He felt at home and one with Alaska.

John "Redds" Cooper started this fishing guide many years ago, much like an ocean bright salmon begins his journey. His ideas for the project were vivid and exciting. Redds love and extensive knowledge of the outdoors, especially salmon species, coupled with his wife Jillian's photography and writing skills made them the perfect pair to write this guide.

Completing this book to share his knowledge of salmon and Alaska became Redd's lifelong dream. Upon his passing, Jillian took up the torch to finish this masterpiece and bring it back home. Then an amazing thing happened, I befriended my grandson, Jack. While Jillian finished this guide, we spent the summer fishing together for salmon. Our quest was to catch the Salmon Slam – all five species of salmon.

After spending decades here in Alaska, I learned that salmon fishing isn't all about the catching. It's the quest – the joy is in the journey. I hope through the pages of this book you will learn the ins-and-outs of fishing techniques and flies for the different salmon species, but most importantly, I hope you enjoy your salmon fishing journey. Appreciate the time you spend fishing with others, and the gift they give you to become part of their lives. Forgive them for their faults and bad casts, as they will forgive you. Be willing to learn from others, even your grandson. Then pass your knowledge and passion onto someone else.

Be 'Salmon Strong' and cast on! ...and if you ever reach the Kenai Peninsula, ask for Fly Bob.

Fly Bob Cooper,

Kenai & Russian River Fishing Guide

Cooper Landing, Alaska

I flipped to the back of the book and saw that Mom had taped in two pictures. The first was Dad's photo of the "Kenai Kids" and alongside was our version of the "Kenai Kids II." I studied both pictures and reflected on all the faces.

I thought about what Fly Bob said about the salmon's journey. We all have a journey and have to follow where it leads us.

Dad had his. Mom has hers. Fly Bob has his, and I have mine. Yet, we're all entwined somehow...like salmon.

Inside the middle of the book, Mom placed my cardboard certificate of the Salmon Slam. All the flies hooked into each of their rightful fingers on the traced hand.

Dad would probably be saying something right now like, *"Living is all about cycles."*

I guess he would be right. Night and day, ebb and flow, happiness and sorrow, grief and hope, life and death, we're drifting our flies through all the experiences in between. Eventually, like the salmon runs, all things come around again. Even though he's gone, the cycle doesn't have to end.

What a summer! What a journey, and it's just beginning!

I wonder what next summer brings.

Slipping the book into my pack, I filled my lungs with fresh air and smiled.

A brook trout swirled over by a submerged log, leaving only ripples behind. I slowly reached for my fly line and knotted a Caribou Hair Caddis at the end of my tippet. After a perfect roll cast, I sat by the water's edge and waited patiently for a fish to rise.

CAST OF SALMON

Pacific or Alaskan Salmon are born in a freshwater stream as eggs and then spend most of their adult lives in the ocean's salt water. Using their olfactory (or sense of smell), they find their way back home and return to their birth stream to spawn or reproduce. The salmon spawn only once and die soon afterward. Their scientific genus name *Oncorhynchus* means "hooked snout."

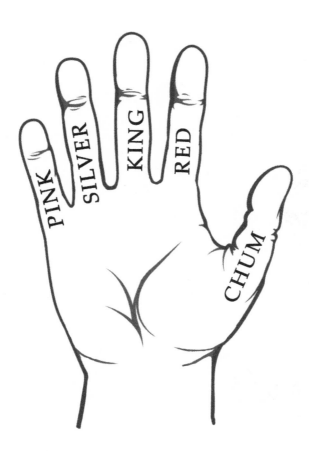

FLY RECIPES

These are some of the Alaskan fly patterns mentioned within the story, some even suggested by the real Fly Bob himself! Fly tiers use "recipes" to tie them in different styles such as streamers, nymphs, dries, and flesh/egg imitations. You can tie them using a multitude of materials, colors, and sizes for whatever species of salmon, trout, or fish species you are targeting.

EVERGLOW FLY

HOOK: #0-3

THREAD: Chartreuse

BODY: Fluorescent Green Everglow tubing

HACKLE: Chartreuse Saddle Hackle

KRYSTAL WOOLLY BUGGER

HOOK: 3X Streamer, #4

THREAD: 6/0 Black

TAIL: Black Marabou

BODY: Black Chenille

HACKLE: Saddle Hackle

SIDES: Krystal Flash

PINK WOG

HOOK: #2 Mouse Hook

THREAD: 6/0 Pink

TAIL: Pink Marabou, Purple Flashabou

BODY: Deer Hair, pink and red alternated and trimmed

ALASKAN EXPRESS (EGG SUCKING LEECH)

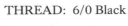

HOOK: #2-#4

THREAD: 6/0 Black

TAIL: Purple Marabou

BODY: Purple chenille over lead wire

HACKLE: Purple saddle hackle

EGG HEAD: Fluorescent pink/red chenille ball

ELK HAIR CADDIS

HOOK: #8-18

THREAD: 3/0 Tan

BODY: Hare's Ear dubbing

HACKLE: Brown Saddle Hackle

WING: Natural Elk Hair

FLESH FLY

HOOK: #2-#4

THREAD: Black

BODY: White marabou twisted and wrapped forward

WING: White marabou from body tied back (Also can be tied with a rabbit strip)

FLY RECIPES CONTINUED

COHO FLY

HOOK: #4

THREAD: Black

WING: Red over White Bucktail

BLACK BEAR NYMPH

HOOK: #6-#16

THREAD: Black

TAIL: Black Bear guard hair

BODY: Black Bear underfur

HACKLE: Black Bear guard hairs

THORAX: Black Bear underfur

FLASH FLY

HOOK: Size #2 - #6

THREAD: 6/0 Red

TAIL: Silver Poly Flash

BODY: Silver Poly Flash

WING: Silver Flashabou

HACKLE: Red saddle hackle

POLAR BEAR NYMPH

HOOK: #6-#18

THREAD: White

TAIL: Polar Bear guard hair/White calf tail

BODY: Polar Bear underfur or white dubbing

THORAX: Polar Bear underfur or white dubbing

HACKLE: Polar Bear guard fur or white calf tail

COTTON CANDY

HOOK: #6-#12

THREAD: 6/0 Peach/Pink

TAIL: Glo Bug Yarn – cotton candy

BODY: Peach Chenille

WING: Glo Bug Yarn – cotton candy

PHEASANT TAIL NYMPH

HOOK: #12-20

THREAD: Tan

TAIL: Pheasant Tail Fibers

BODY: Pheasant Tail Fibers

RIBBING: Fine gold wire

WINGCASE: Ringneck Pheasant Tail Fibers

THORAX: Peacock Herl

FLY RECIPES CONTINUED

POLAR SHRIMP

HOOK: #2-#6

THREAD: 6/0 Black

TAIL: Red Hackle

BODY: Orange Chenille

HACKLE: Orange saddle hackle

WING: White polar bear or white calf hair

DIRTY BUNNY

HOOK: #2-#8

THREAD: 6/0 Thread

TAIL: Marabou

BODY: Light Brown/Grizzly Ginger Rabbit Strip

HEAD: Egg color chenille

CONEHEAD POPSICLE

HOOK: #2-#8

THREAD: 3/0 Black

HACKLE: Marabou – fluorescent orange, red, and purple

BODY: Mylar tinsel

FLASH: Flashabou

"Be at the right place at the right time,
with the right fly, the right techniques,
and the right attitude,
...and you'll be a fine fisherman."

-John "Redds" Cooper

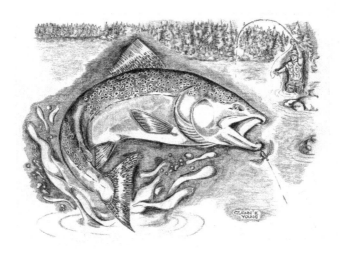

"That's the life of a salmon, born in freshwater,
head out to the ocean for a few years,
and then come back to their birth stream to mate.
Then they die."

-Fly Bob

BIBLIOGRAPHY & RESOURCES

Children's Grief Awareness:
www.childrengrieve.org/find-support

Official State of Alaska Vacation and Travel Information:
www.travelalaska.com

Alaska Department of Fish and Game (ADF&G):
www.adfg.state.ak.us

ADF&G (Animals' Page):
www.adfg.alaska.gov/index.cfm?adfg=animals.main

Fish Alaska Magazine: www.fishalaskamagazine.com

Trout Unlimited: www.tu.org

Save Our Wild Salmon: www.wildsalmon.org

ARTISTS:

Sheila Dunn: https://www.sheiladunnart.com/

Nick Cobler: https://nickcobler.com/

Glenn K. Young: https://digitalmedia.fws.gov/digital/collection/natdiglib/id/888/rec/2

Timothy Knepp: https://digitalmedia.fws.gov/digital/collection/natdiglib/id/28746/rec/1

Timothy Knepp: https://digitalmedia.fws.gov/digital/collection/natdiglib/id/28745/rec/90

Timothy Knepp: https://digitalmedia.fws.gov/digital/collection/natdiglib/id/6030/rec/14

ACKNOWLEDGEMENTS

As in Fly Bob's Foreword, I began this story much like a juvenile salmon goes out to the ocean and then after many years, faces obstacles, and journeys back home.

While camping through Alaska with my wife years ago, spending time in the Land of the Midnight Sun caught my heart and soul, and I couldn't wait to draft a fishing story about the Salmon Slam. With more summer fishing trips to Alaska, tough losses in life, and refinement of my writing craft, Jack's journey developed and grew into much more.

Thanks to all of these people (and more) who've made a difference in my journey.

To the wonderful Alaskans I've met along the way and the salmon which we caught together – you inspired this book.

To my wife Megan – Thanks for enjoying the mountaintops and weathering the valleys together to always get us back home. This will be the last draft of Survivor I ask you to proofread and edit!

To my three A's, Aaron, Aleia, & Zander – From A to Z, thanks for being the rocks that line the stream to my heart and the waterfalls of laughter.

To my mom (Dianne) and dad (John) – Thanks for your strength, love, and a home stream in which to always return.

To my other family members (The Baumans, The Millers, The Shanes, The Masts, The Arnolds, The Marks, The Pennellas, and The Klines) – Thanks for always being the guides in my life.

To my North Allegheny students, parents, teammates, colleagues, administration, and NA family (Ingomar Middle, McKnight Elementary & Bradford Woods Elementary) – Thanks for encouraging me, not only as an educator but as a lifelong learner.

ACKNOWLEDGEMENTS continued

To all my angling friends (Penn's Woods West TU and PATU) and the fishing guides along my angling adventures, both past and present – Thanks for creating great memories with me on great waters and may we have more to come.

To Relevant Publishing LLC (Sharon, Linda, and the editing team) – Thanks for sharing your talents and guiding me in what makes Alaska authentic and unique.

To my writing friends at the Highlights Foundation, the Western PA SCBWI group, and the Pennsylvania Outdoor Writer's Association (POWA) (Kelly, Kim, Clara, Elizabeth, Brad, and others) – Thanks for sharpening my writing skills and my courage during the Hero's Journey.

To the real 'Fly Bob' – Thanks for being my Alaskan brother and the greatest angler, fly tier, and guide that I know.

What can you do to protect, conserve, and enhance salmon and trout fisheries?

Learn more about salmon and trout by joining and donating to organizations, such as *Trout Unlimited, Save Our Wild Salmon, Wild Salmon Center*, and others who champion for cold, clean water and healthy habitat for fish and wildlife. Visit amazing places where wild salmon are present and support local businesses and native tribal organizations that support conservation efforts. Get involved in volunteering to help your local watersheds by planting trees, picking up waste, monitoring a stream, or even buying a fishing license. Teach others about the amazing life cycle of salmon and share your ideas on how to help them with your parents, friends, and neighbors.

CPSIA information can be obtained
at www.ICGtesting.com
Printed in the USA
BVHW040900110922
646361BV00004B/24